my little war

my little war
louis paul boon

translated by paul vincent

Dalkey Archive Press
Champaign / London

Originally published in Flemish as *Mijn kleine oorlog* by De Arbeiderspers, 1947
Copyright © 1947 by De Arbeiderspers
Translation copyright © 2010 by Paul Vincent
First English translation, 2010

Library of Congress Cataloging-in-Publication Data

Boon, Louis Paul.
  [Mijn kleine oorlog. English.]
  My little war / Louis Paul Boon ; translated by Paul Vincent.
    p. cm.
  Translated from the Flemish.
  ISBN 978-1-56478-558-9 (pbk. : alk. paper)
  1. World War, 1939-1945--Belgium--Fiction. I. Vincent, Paul (Paul F.) II. Title.
PT6407.B57M5513 2009
839.31'364--dc22
               2009033077

Partially funded by the University of Illinois at Urbana-Champaign, as well as by
grants from the National Endowment for the Arts, a federal agency, and the Illinois
Arts Council, a state agency

The translation of this book is funded by the Flemish Literature Fund (Vlaams
Fonds voor de Letteren—www.flemishliterature.be)

www.dalkeyarchive.com

Cover: design and composition by Danielle Dutton, illustration by Nicholas Motte
Printed on permanent/durable acid-free paper and bound in the
United States of America

contents

My Little War 9

Translator's Note 123

You write your Little War.

You'd rather write a different book—grander, deeper, more beautiful. You'd say "these are the curses and prayers of the little man in the face of the big war, these are the songs, this is THE BIBLE OF THE WAR." And then the next day you'd like nothing better than to smash your pen to pieces—an exhilarating feeling—but then the day after that you'd have to go buy a new one—because you've just got to write, it's a natural urge. One man curses till he blows a fuse, another bangs his head against brick walls.

You write your Little War.

The Book about the War

A little writer writes his little war but what great writer will rise up now and present us with his Book About the Great War—with capital letters? But "present" is far too proper a word for such a book. Sling it in our faces, hurl it at our dismayed consciences would be nearer the truth.

Perhaps you'll do it, you who've lost all your worldly goods, as they say, but who as a human being have lost much more, having been evacuated like so much livestock and deported like a criminal, bombed and machine-gunned and toyed with like an empty can being kicked around by a bunch of kids, who've died a hundred times over, mutilated gagged and teeth knocked out with a wrench, so that, sitting there like Job with his boils, you . . . No, sitting there like little Frans Wauters, whose job it was to deliver letters to foreign laborers in Kassel in Germany and who during an air raid took cover down a drain and who when he came out could no longer see Kassel . . . If they'd slid a chair under my trembling legs as I sat there I could have surveyed all-that-had-once-been-Kassel . . . And so sitting there on that chair and looking at what-had-once-been-the-world, you'd be able to write the book that we might not have found the courage to read, or about which we might say: I don't understand it . . . because we're used to reading words stuck together with lifeless characters and are only able to appreciate something when, as they say, it has rhythm, but no meaning. Because you'd write words born of sweat and mud and dying horses in an upturned wagon and blocks of houses torn apart by the blast, and blood. With those words you'd construct sentences like twisted rails that start out perfectly normal but soon twist up into the air, as if the bombed trains were straining to take off into the sky but when the rails ended crashed back to earth. You'd make sentences like arms extended in pity but faltering halfway because pity's not appropriate here . . . because if our hands don't kill we'll be killed ourselves, our books will be burned and our paintings condemned as degenerate and our finest thoughts regarded as the thoughts of madmen, and all that's left will be the thoughts of sadists and medieval heretic-burners. And your bloody words, strung together into painfully contorted sentences, will form pages like fields strewn with mines and churned up by tanks, like the silent and still faintly smoldering cities of Warsaw Coventry Hamburg Kharkov Rotterdam and the whole of Russia which they tried to make us believe was inhabited entirely by sluts who ate their own children and men who ran around with knives between their clenched teeth.

Oh your book would be a book of concentrated tears and bloodlust and *schweinerei*, the stuff that doesn't belong in any book because people nowadays turn up their noses when even the slightest little f—k defaces the page, but in Your Book that sort of thing will stand as a flaming testimony to the beast that's conquered the human spirit. Your book, which you only wrote to escape your mute pain and blind fear and so as not to go mad, your book will be the mirror the abyss the hell that later generations will come to look at—perhaps after paying ten cents' admission, like at the museum, since there'll still be profiteers around then too—so as . . . oh, so as to what? To start all over again perhaps. To say of your book, as they murder and rape and spread their lies, that it's the most enormous lie ever written. To excommunicate you from the holy church and put you on the list of banned books and throw you on a new bonfire and whoop round it like Red Indians. Because I, a little writer, have little enemies who sling mud, but you, great writer, will have great enemies who will desecrate your memory even unto the seventh generation.

Where are the days when you struggled to pay off the mortgage on your house, sometimes making a little headway as a day laborer and sometimes scrambling backwards, having to join the unemployment line. And one morning your wife says: feel, there's something moving. And then on cue the policeman's there with your draft papers—and so your wife will just have to pay off the house by herself, and she sends you packages and writes letters, for instance one day: I can't feel anything moving now, do you think something's wrong? And then the next: oh thank god, it's turned round again!

And meanwhile you're getting one franc's pay a day and someone steals the butter and the officers are reeling around drunk and war breaks out—just when you're stuck there on the Albert Canal and they're right there staring at you, the gray bastards—and you're left to pick up the pieces. Your child must be starting to walk about now, but you don't know for sure. You don't even know if your wife has any taxes to pay, yes or no—and besides THE BOMBS ARE FALLING *maybe she's already dead back there*

BOOM

that was close!

And to think that that huge mob of people stationed there on the Albert Canal were all still clinging to the crazy notion that these were just some especially elaborate maneuvers.

The Goldfish

I knew Van den Abeele was lying there with his shoulder torn open, but I still didn't look, I turned to the lieutenant of the 9th, who was standing there on the little cobbled road, arms open wide, railing at them: *saligauds, boches*! As if they could hear him on the other side of the Albert Canal. There was plenty of other noise anyway. Right next to us someone was emptying the belt of his machine gun, he was sitting on a chair he'd brought from the dairy and who knows maybe it all just looked like the national shooting range to him. Except for the dive-bombers, that is. And except that we were dying of thirst. Bah, said the radio operator, it's all down to fate, if it's your turn to die, you die. What's-his-name replied that more people were dying here in one goddamn hour than over the course of ten years back in his village. Whereupon the radio operator shrugged his shoulders and started explaining to me that it was OUR FATE, no one died in your village because it was their fate to come and die here. And What's-his-name was about to reply when those fucking Stukas came screaming and rat-tat-tatting down on us again, it was unbearable. The two from the field hospital cursed and said that they couldn't be in every damn place at once. I'm bleeding myself, said the fattest of the two. No, it was unbearable, especially with those senseless orders. Get some more ammunition, said the lieutenant and there was no more ammunition to get, it had blown sky high half an hour ago. And try to bring me back a loaf of bread, Louis, he said. Yes, he'd joined us as a simple corporal out of basic training and every year when we had to go back to camp for more drilling he was a little higher in rank and he looked down on us a little more arrogantly, but when he was in trouble he'd still say Louis in that old friendly way. A loaf of bread, as though he didn't know that the field kitchen had gone the way of the ammunition. But we went anyway, if we could get away from that dike for a bit we couldn't hear them over there shouting *VORWÄRTS* so loud. I looked at What's-his-name to ask if he was coming too and at that very moment the radio operator passed the long-awaited message to the lieutenant: every man for himself. We started smashing everything up with axes like lunatics, the machine-gunner even made matchwood of his chair, and we tried to retreat along the cobbled road but it was already under fire. Bryske, who counted to 3 and then ran across as fast as he could, fell head over heels on the other side. So we had to go straight through the dairy and What's-his-name smashed the window open with the butt of his rifle, and there was a glass bowl behind it that rolled over. We crawled through the window in order to bash the front door in, but all of a sudden What's-his-name stopped and started biting his fingernails. I saw him pick up the bowl that had gotten caught between the window frame and the curtains; he filled it with water and carefully put it back in its place. And because I was waiting for him, he gave me an infuriated look, as if I'd done something wrong, heaven knows what. A bit further on we had to throw ourselves flat on our faces since that bunch from the other side had now crossed the Canal, and I didn't really have the nerve to look back, because it was an inferno now. And in our ditch What's-his-name said: imagine you lived in that dairy, and got back after you'd had to run away, wouldn't you be glad to see that your goldfish were still alive? Well? . . . Why did you make that awful face at me?

And I had to laugh. It wasn't me making that awful face, I said, it was you.

Actually, I made those goldfish up, that's what stories are for. But this isn't made up: What's-his-name had to crawl through a gap in the hedge with his pistol over his shoulder, and he got caught. We shouted at him to cut the leather strap but he didn't hear us, he just stood there in the line of fire and shit himself.

Whereas What's-his-name, on the other hand—oh, a different What's-his-name of course—stood astride our ditch and emptied one magazine after another—he was completely berserk.

And me? Oh, I sat gnawing on my fingernails, observing everything and trying to keep my thoughts from running off to the insane asylum. Do you suppose they're already dropping bombs

BACK THERE? *I wondered—oh god, goddamn don't let them die, let them see me 1 more time—*WHAT'S THE USE OF HAVING A KID AND THEN DYING BEFORE YOU EVER GET TO SEE IT?

Prosper tells a story: a guy had one eye blown out and when he was taken to the military doctor's shelter, the doctor was just getting ready to leave—we had to drive him back into the shelter at bayonet-point to make him treat that eye first.

By the roadside: two stretcher-bearers with arms spread wide and an overturned stretcher with its 4 arms spread wide and its dying occupant lying next to it, BOMBED A SECOND TIME.

And two soldiers who'd made a run for it on the Albert Canal were picked up by gendarmes who'd also run for it and were brought before a court-martial on a church square chaired by a general who shouted the whole time and wore slippers—and suddenly the German planes were there and the general leaped into a car in his slippers and drove off, shouting THEY WOULD BE COURT-MARTIALED LATER.

And speaking of the general, my wife told me a while later that a whole bunch of those old men with red bands round their caps had driven past our house, that they were all too worn out to fight anymore but had big beautiful dogs with them and young girls of around sixteen or so.

The Border

Since that bunch over there controlled the high ground, their fire swept the plateau we had to cross—and where we first, crawling on our hands and knees, had to cut through our own barbed wire. Seen from the ditch it looked like a stampeded herd jostling around the barbed wire tearing the clothes off their backs. Some shouted at them to get down. It's all because there's no officer around, shouted someone else. And that was true. All through the mobilization period you couldn't take one wrong step without one of them staring daggers. What's-his-name and I were once put up on charges for falling asleep on sentry duty by a pile of stupid turf. But here we hadn't seen any officers after the first shot was fired, except that poor lieutenant from the 9th, but what good was a lieutenant against that bunch over there? But since we'd started looking for food and ammunition, we were getting to know the area better than our own kit bags; we moved in an arc round the barbed wire and reached the main road a little earlier—at least we would have got there earlier if we hadn't seen those gray-painted vehicles on their treads. A little brat of a soldier was leaning out of one, and funnily enough it looked like he was shaking his fist at us. And immediately thereafter, a few yards from us, that ghostly lieutenant from the 9th crawled out of our ditch, threw his revolver away, and put his hands up. And it's possible that What's-his-name said "come on," or equally possible that I said it, but we both threw our rifles away and stood up next to the lieutenant. And what about that little brat of a soldier in his black uniform? He laughed and said he was 18 and had fought in Poland and Spain. But Spain . . . that was probably a bluff. He got out his ersatz cigarettes and offered us one. He said that we had to keep going, *immer weiter*, and stretched out his arm towards the main road. His fist was still clenched, I looked at it and then understood why he'd pointed it at us, there was a little revolver hidden in it. Later What's-his-name asked me: did you see this and did you see that, but I think I walked along with my eyes shut, because I couldn't look at all those horses and people and children lying there in their own stench. And as kids they'd told us at school that the road to hell is a road of darkness, and I'd immediately recognized that road when I saw it. Do you have any idea where we are? asked What's-his-name. I looked and all I saw was a flat expanse covered with rubble. This may be where that café was the day before yesterday where they had that nice pickup truck. And this is where the baker's was with those three hot-blooded daughters. The day before yesterday it had been the village of Veltwezelt and now it was nothing. One of the three daughters, the youngest and I think the prettiest, was lying there with . . . but I'd rather forget that as quickly as possible. And on the threshold of the ex-café lay two Germans. Just as though they'd drunk themselves stupid, said What's-his-name, but I couldn't make myself laugh. We followed the main road towards the border where there was a fencepost and beyond that pole a different country and a different people. A farmer came out with a bucket of water and he said that if we were thirsty we could drink. I looked at the farmer, and you'll laugh, but he looked just like the Flemish writer Stijn Streuvels.

So what if that farmer was the spitting image of Stijn Streuvels? You may think I'm trying to make the point that the people from Germany could just as well have been the people from Belgium, but really, I'm not—he looked like him, that's all—and I still don't know if the people there were the same as us, we didn't see anything but bits of meadow surrounded by barbed wire, and fat women who came from a long way off to look at us as we stood there naked to be checked for lice—apart from that we saw S.S. officers who did nothing but count and count and count again, and apart from that we were hungry, and apart from that we GOT lice but by then there were no more inspections.

Hallucination

Have you looked at Voncke, What's-his-name asked me, as we lay in the dormitory with our arms under our heads looking at the stuff the Poles had carved in the wood of the beds. Sure, we were all thin, we were all hungry, but Voncke was a terrible sight. His eyes were sinking into his face like leaves on water, but getting enormous, looking too big for his skull. He was on the top bunk in the corner, on the straw and lice left behind by the Poles. I turned away from all that Polish carving, since apart from something that looked like "Viva America" I couldn't make head or tail of it anyway, and looked at Voncke. He was higher up than we were and was staring over us into the distance, I followed his gaze and at first had the stupid idea that he might be watching a bird in flight and dreaming of freedom, since I was just a sentimental chump. But it wasn't a bird, he was staring at Kitchen III, with its German soldier pacing up and down by the barbed wire as if being a sentry were some great honor. But Voncke couldn't even see the sentry, and he couldn't have been thinking about home, it had to be something quite different. And then, that night when he stared with sunken eyes at something he couldn't see, he sang. It was a song we'd all learned at school—there wasn't much to those school songs, but when Voncke sang them, oh Christ, you could have cried your eyes out and made a real fool of yourself. I looked round the dormitory and saw everyone listening with phony smiles on their lips and then one of them finally said: hey Voncke, why haven't they put you on the radio yet? He laughed and to tell the truth that was the saddest thing of all. They decided to play a joke on him—or at least what passes as a joke in Belgium: if you ask a farmer the way to Nieuwkerken, he flails his arms like a windmill and sends you to Woubrechtegem. And so they asked Voncke if he'd do a cabaret evening in the dormitory. He did it, he got up on the bench and sang about the smith in his smithy who hammered clop clop clop, and they asked him why he didn't dance to that clop clop clop of his, and so he did that too, and they said he'd make a good tap dancer and then he leaped around and stamped on the wooden floor of the barracks in his worn-out military boots.

I couldn't bear the sight any longer and leaned out the window of the latrine to look out at the heath over the barbed wire. And a little later Voncke arrived. He hoisted himself over the latrine and groped around in the dark before sinking back, discouraged. Are you looking for something? I asked. He mumbled something and tried to get away, but I stopped him and started to talk about his village, which I'd been to, about the girls there, who were quite notorious—because when you left the dance hall with them in the gathering Saturday dusk, they pounced on you of their own accord—and in the same breath I asked: were you looking for something there above the latrine? He stared at me with his sunken eyes and I could tell from his lower lip, trembling and trembling, that he was ready to open up. I dreamed about it, he said, I saw it so clearly in my dream: there was a 5th of a loaf on the shelf above the latrine, and I came to take a look.

We sent cards: POW mail badly wounded lightly wounded in good health DELETE WHAT DOES NOT APPLY—and we received a card back to say all was well with them back there, no damage to the house, the baby can already run like a deer, he's already trampled the leeks in the garden.

Oh said someone, we'll have some stories to tell when we get home—and we got home and had nothing to tell about, everyone was talking about the Mass Exodus of civilians and all the young girls were walking around with bandages round their legs as if it were the latest fashion and all the women were lining at the food distribution centers and sometimes fainting from hunger.

Did you miss the Mass Exodus entirely then, since you were captured after only three days? they asked—and I hurried home in shame to where the baby, who had trampled all the leeks, was afraid of my threadbare greatcoat and my beard and my very skinny face. I gave him "the prisoner of war" as a present, a figure that I'd carved back there with a blunt knife from a block of wood. He smashed it to bits and cried and hid behind his mother.

Red Night

Then there was that night when the sirens wailed again and almost out of habit my wife said: you get the little one right away and go into the garden, I'll come out after you with a blanket—I think she'd say as much in her sleep—oh, that night, hold my typewriter tight, keep me from getting sentimental . . .

I pushed them into the pit next door and pulled the blanket over their heads and prepared to die. Just then the first flare was dropped, over there, a long way behind the terrace of the workers' houses, and another look, look, and another. They're marking out the railway line, I said. But was it the railway? There were already red flares above our house and behind it and in front of it, we had a bloodred house and the terrace of the workers' houses was a bloodred terrace. It had become a toy town. Is it really the railway they're marking out? asked my wife, and my son echoed her: is it the railway, Dad? Yes, I said and all the while my heart was in my mouth. And then Staf Spies and his wife and Mathilde with her children and the Protestant and the whole of the poor district who didn't have cellars came looking for shelter in the pit, which was the basement of the house they were building next to ours. Staf Spies, who on other nights sat around smoking and giving a running commentary ("look at that and listen to that"), watched and said nothing. Now he simply saw, and was silent. He held a glowing cigarette in one red hand and tried to stop his fingers from shaking. I thought we'd had it, something I've thought before, actually, like when the plank shot out from underneath me high on the scaffolding and the petroleum lamp exploded in the factory. But that doesn't matter now, I threw myself in the pit and put my head under the blanket and heard my son say: and deliver us from evil amen. My wife got annoyed that it was taking so long, why don't they just drop them already, she said. Yes that was it, drop and die, but we couldn't go on dying all through that red night. I crawled out of the hole and looked round, there was a fire over in the marshaling yards and we hadn't even heard them dropping. The planes left and the red tried valiantly to stay red, but a long way in the distance the night had turned back to what it always is, black with twinkling stars. And quiet, so quiet that suddenly, far away, I don't know where, you could hear the bombs falling.

Staf Spies and his wife and Mathilde and the whole neighborhood who had been with us in the basement space emerged and each one of them was babbling louder than the next. They're hitting Kortrijk now, said Staf Spies who was listening with his head cocked to one side. Where? asked Mathilde absently, though she'd heard perfectly well. Kortrijk, he repeated and the whole twinkling night was full of the word Kortrijk. And I thought of Kortrijk, of What's-his-name who had been a prisoner of war with me and whom I had written a very cagey letter and who had told me in reply that he was lame and was stuck in a chair with a brace on his legs, and I wondered how he would have got down into our pit with that brace on.

When the people who had fled into the fields came back—who'd endured even greater terrors than we had out there, because, they whispered, paratroopers had landed—Staf Spies said: the world's been spared again for today. Because Staf Spies's world is the terrace of the workers' houses and Kortrijk isn't part of that, it's another world. A long line of lamps run by hand generators made its way through the gardens in the red night that had become a black night again. Only a train was still burning over in the marshaling yards.

And among a mass of people rounded up and machine-gunned by the Germans, one survivor who'd dropped a second too soon lay for hours among the dead without daring to move—at night when it's dark he crawled out and hid in the cesspit, with only his head sticking out.

And Mrs. Lammens who doesn't have two pennies left to rub together and who says the war will be over next week has a fight with her husband on Sunday night because of his pipe, which he asked her to knock the ash out of onto their front step—and Mrs. Lammens knocks the ash out but by accident the last bit of tobacco as well, and her husband gets up in a rage and smashes his pipe to bits, and something snaps in Mrs. Lammens's head and she drops dead.

And the brother of that cripple from Thrift Street who's been to Germany to work and then came home with a wife, a German woman, that German wife won't let him go back, she says things are bad over there in Germany, the regime and what have you—because all her neighbors in Thrift Street are anti-German.

Old Magpie

There was one guy we called Magpie, a little guy with a birdlike neck and a sharp hooked nose and goddamn crafty eyes, but they should have called him Rat because he was infinitely more like one of those—Magpie had always been a Flemish activist and for a while had even been a member of the Fascist Party and could be seen strutting through the town, a magpie in a black uniform with a leather strap across his shoulder. But that was only when they were dripping with money at home, as soon as he was down on his luck again he did quite the opposite and was happy to speak French and shout Up with the Socialists and even sing *we'll keep the red flag flying here*, if anyone would buy him a pint or help him get a job. He didn't need to earn a lot, just so long as he got the chance to practice his trade and then come back at night and like a rat make off with whatever he'd set aside for himself during the day. Once when he was caught red-handed he fell to the ground and wept and howled and called himself the most wretched person in the whole world and while he was doing that he took off his belt, which was thick as a bull-whip, then jumped up and lashed out at the people surrounding him, cutting their faces open.

That was Magpie and his father was Old Magpie, who could easily have been called Old Rat, who was worth millions one day and buying drinks for everyone and the next day was facing one lawsuit after another for smashing up a café, sexually assaulting a woman, or covering some political group's meeting room—not the Flemish nationalists' meeting room—with pitch, and then the following morning woke up in a brothel or in jail without a penny to his name. So that Magpie, Young Magpie, when he asked for his pocket money, never knew whether he'd get a thousand francs or a kick in the ass. Now the Germans were here, and really people shouldn't go around saying that all Flemish nationalists were in the pay of the Germans even before the war, that's not true: Old Magpie was terribly upset when war broke out because he didn't have any tobacco to roll himself a cigarette, and hadn't been able to buy himself a pint for four days. He went to work on an airfield on the outskirts of Brussels with a spade and a knapsack made out of an old piece of baize from a card table. There was still a cigarette ad on the baize that had become his knapsack. And as he leaned on his spade there he had the idea of building an airfield like that at his own expense: he had a stolen cement mixer at home and without a second thought he went up to the German with the most gold on his collar and explained his plan. Of course a project like that was risky, you couldn't build an airfield overnight, and the rest of us would start worrying that the war might suddenly end and we'd be left holding the baby—something Old Magpie never considered, for the simple reason that that's how it had been all his life: one day the world, the next nothing. But the war went on and on thank God and the airfield was finished and Old Magpie was able to collect his money. He put on his best clothes and was given a voucher in Brussels to collect his money in Leuven, he was a millionaire—how many times did that make? And of course he had to celebrate all evening and into the early hours in Leuven, he was in a bedroom in a brothel sleeping it off and so didn't hear the sirens wailing or see the red flares falling. The bombs rained down on Leuven, there was thunder and lightning, and waking up in utter bewilderment he saw the walls collapsing and the roof crashing down in flames—and by some miracle he was the only one left alive, sitting there shivering among the dead whores. He'd lost his millions and he'd lost his pants and was dressed in nothing but an overcoat that wasn't his and was covered in blood and when he went home they barely recognized him. Have you come to see Dad? asked Young Magpie . . . in that case you'll have to come back later, because Dad's gone to Leuven to get his money. And Old Magpie kicked his son aside to go look in the mirror, where he found that in the course of one night he'd grown old and gray.

Someone tells us that the Germans flood their prison cells with water and the prisoners have to bail them out with whatever they happen to have handy, and if they have nothing handy, then with their hands—and this someone has scarcely left the house when Gaston's wife comes in and says Gaston's in jail and has asked her to bring him a mop BECAUSE YOU KNOW WHAT A STICK-LER FOR CLEANLINESS HE IS, *she says.*

And Josie who was picked up for smuggling butter and was cooped up with three or four women in the same cell, where they all had to use the same bucket, tells us that she thought she caught a glimpse of Liesje—she glanced over the railing and saw someone who looked just like Liesje, but her head was too heavily bandaged TO SAY FOR SURE.

And it says in the German papers that two guys who were informed on and arrested were hanged—but it doesn't say they were actually hung up by their feet TILL THEY DIED.

Van den Borre

Now take Van den Borre who always wore wooden clogs and who's dead now and forgotten and not even buried, bits of him were just swept up and shoved in the ground, his name and his case are typical of these times.

Van den Borre stood in the unemployment line in the mornings and in the afternoon went down the main road with a wooden box containing a brush and a coal shovel, and when his box was full of horse manure, he sold it to people who had gardens. Of course, he didn't make as much of a profit as you, for instance, an honest citizen who works and cheats and saves and worries and perhaps lies awake half the night thinking about how you're going to work and cheat and worry and save the next day. But he had an easier time of it and hung around Lazy Corner. He held forth about things he'd read in the paper but only half understood and had already half forgotten (before the war he'd subscribed to the socialist magazine *Forward* and during the war to the German magazine *Forward* and never saw the slightest difference between them), and he was only frightened of one thing: of receiving a summons as he had during 1914–1918 when he refused to work and then they'd almost beaten him to death when he dutifully showed up at the police station.

But he wouldn't talk about this war. The fact that the other people had made a run for it and been machine-gunned and bombed on the road, that wasn't his concern. He did, it's true, nod in agreement when anyone started talking about the Mass Exodus, but he thought mainly of himself—after all, why should he think mainly of others? But when his daughter got married and all he could contribute to the wedding party were 3 smuggled ration loaves without any butter or filling, and the brothels next to the station were bombed so that the slivers of glass flew out as far as our street, he started finally talking about this war too. It's getting bad now, he said. I looked at him and it was true, it was getting bad: he was so poor his knees were poking through his pants and his eyes were bulging out of his head with hunger. And suddenly he disappeared from Lazy Corner . . . I was sitting on the pavement one Saturday afternoon and he walked past with knees wobbling slightly as usual, his head nodding along with his body and his pipe nodding along with his head. Afternoon, he said and I could tell he'd come a long way. Germany? I asked. He sat down next to me. No, he said, he'd been in Wallonia, in Florennes, and of course he didn't earn as much as the ones in Germany, but he got to come home every two weeks and bought rolling tobacco which sold like hotcakes down there. And by the way, did I know where he could buy some leek seed? And, as far as work, they were building a concrete runway down there, and they were lucky to have their spades to lean on because otherwise they'd keel over from sheer laziness. And he laughed. A German had said to him: shoulder to the wheel now, Fan ten Porre. And he replied: don't worry, I won't stop it turning! But the main thing is—and he took his pipe out of his mouth and waved it in the air—but the main thing is: there's no bombing down there. And he looked down at his feet with his nodding head to hide his silent laughter.

And then they did bomb down there all of a sudden and Van den Borre, leaning on his spade so as not to keel over, was more or less rammed into the ground. His wife handed me a mourning card: died as a result of military action in Florennes, May 9, 1944; he had loved his work and had been taken from us (every bit of him) exactly where no one was expecting it. And she told me that a policeman had come to ask if she was Van den Borre's wife and tell her that her husband was lying wounded in Florennes. And she had put her black shawl over her head and gone to the German headquarters to ask for a travel permit to go to Florennes, but at the headquarters they'd said to her: oh, there's no point, you won't find any trace of him.

And there are whispers everywhere about the Resistance and the White Brigade—which isn't so much a White Brigade as a red army that's in action day and night but won't accomplish one damn thing for their trouble, neither now nor after the war, and in fact will be in just as much danger then of getting thrown in jail.

And Maurice and Roger with his slight lisp, who are both in that red army, have discovered a German soldier who says he's a communist and sings revolutionary songs with them—but when he's on sentry duty at the gate of the barracks still won't let them in, orders are orders, he says.

Yes, and a German is still a German, replies Maurice.

And Roger's mother lives next to the fuel depot, which the English attack, but they don't hit the depot, they hit the terrace of the workers' houses right next to it, and now one is dead and one is half-dead and the one who escaped as if by a miracle is standing there shouting: you can't make an omelet without breaking some eggs.

Small-Time Coal Thieves

Description of Black Corner: a red light in the darkness on a suspension bridge across a breathtakingly black stretch of water, next to the bombed-out cement works, a section of which juts into the gray sky with a useless window-opening still in it, and next to the railway repair shop, which has also been bombed, but whose bomb fell right next to it, in the middle of the road, blowing away all the cobbles—and it's there, beyond the embankment by the repair shop, where the coal is piled up, that we must take our reader, as Hendrik Conscience, our Flemish Dickens, would say . . . but he wouldn't like what he'd find there, because he'd soon run into the coal thieves.

Coal Thief 1: Gateway Henrietta, who, as her name indicates, lives in a gateway. You open the gate and you're in the kitchen, which is odd enough in itself, but you certainly won't find any coal there, it's always gone the same night she steals it. She's pregnant of course and in that state crawls up the embankment and on the other side fills a bag (scrabbling around in the pile with her hands) and then gives the full bag a kick so it rolls back down against the fence below, where her lover—her husband's in Germany—takes care of it. Coal Thief 2: a skinny guy with a cap that's far too big for him pulled down over the darting eyes in his spotty face, and with elbows and knees pushing their way through pant legs and jacket sleeves, and who uses different and more dangerous tactics: he jumps onto moving trains taking the curve under cover of darkness and loosens their sliding doors a little—not too much, because it's anthracite in there, and the whole car would empty out. From there on, it's the same system as Gateway Henrietta's. Coal Thief 3: leader of a gang, each man with a bag and a bike, who all hide behind the ruined walls of the cement works, and he looks round the corner left and he looks round the corner right, and then he says "come on" and the gang descends onto a passing coal truck, each with their own sack and their own bike, after which they go to a café that half burned down in the 1914–1918 war and the rest of which was bombed in this one—but where two hours after every storm everyone's back serving beer again. There it stands with cracked walls and tar-paper windows and a door made of jagged planks.

And then there are the folks from the barracks that aren't barracks but actually the Albert I emergency housing from the last war: a woman with a dirty shopping bag that she took to buy fish with that morning, a woman with a bucket, and a woman with a child on her arm. And then there are women sitting in the ruins of the cement works and biding their time and chatting about the war and sometimes calling out to their kids who are playing among the ruins and likely to fall and cut their heads open: Maria, for Christ's sake stay here where I can see you! And then there are the so-called railway workers who buy old caps from a fireman or an engineer and enter the repair shop through the door in the blank wall marked "staff only" and fill their bags and leave again, jeered at by the women who've been sitting there for hours—what are they waiting for? They're waiting for the guard, who sometimes for a mark or a flash of bare knee will gesture with his head: go on then. And then he stands with his back to the coal as though he's looking high up over there at the gap in the ruined wall.

And last of all there's Flor who comes pulling a handcart, himself between the shafts liked a worn-out horse, his wife pushing on the left and his sister pushing on the right, going as far as the embankment where they all station themselves next to each other and wait—Flor distributes the wrapping paper—since of course they're all deeply fascinated by that stretch of water and that bridge and that red light. Until at a certain hour the night train goes past and the engineer kicks down a pile of briquettes, half of which he'll reclaim the following morning at Flor's place. These are just a few small-time coal thieves. There's no need for us to talk about the big-time thieves, since everybody knows them.

And a woman shouts BOMBS BOMBS *even before they've dropped any, and for God's sake she's right: they really are bombing—and in the deathly silence then, when you can't hear anything but the pounding of your own heart, a cart approaches from a long way down the main road, as though the cart too is running away from something. But no sooner are the planes gone than you hear people babbling as though the whole world's turned into one big farmer's market: blablabla and blablabla, where did all these voices come from all of a sudden? and then the siren sounds the all-clear and all the children start dancing like peace has come. And that's how you can tell that even the children are starting to live from day to day, from hour to hour.*

Tewna

I was taking Industry Street home so as to avoid the high street, because they'd be waiting again round that windy corner to check my papers. Not that they weren't in order, far from it, but it made me feel sick to my stomach, I wouldn't be able to eat again if I ran into them. And going down Industry Street I saw Vieze's wife in her doorway and I heard her shout to Alfred's wife, who was leaning out of an open upstairs window with a feather duster in her hand that there was no milk again and what was she supposed to feed her little ones with, they're not even entitled to an egg these days. And she gave me a furious look, as if the war was my fault. Alfred's wife shouted back from the upstairs window—something about the Germans: that she preferred gray to black. And that too was aimed at me, because she suspected me of being pro-German, because I kept my mouth shut when people talked about the war in our neighborhood. But Vieze's wife couldn't care less, all she could think about were her little ones who were suffering and she planted her fists on her hips then and shouted: let me tell you something, let me . . .

Suddenly the kids were coming out of their nursery school and Vieze's son together with my son rounded the corner with their arms outstretched like the wings of a plane. And while Vieze's son was dropping bombs on the public air-raid shelter—which was full of water and which no one was ever going to crawl into anyway—my son imitated the air-raid siren. He was damn good at it, too. No sooner had he started wailing than one or two doors opened and the people leaned out, all ears. M-m-mommy, said Vieze's son, who couldn't speak too well, th-th-this afternoon we need to bring a cup in, we're having ss-ss-tewna. And, duster in hand, Alfred's wife laughed till it hurt. And, my son's hand in mine, I went home laughing too. But then he also said: dad, we're having tewna at school this afternoon. Stew, I corrected him, you shouldn't imitate Vieze's kid, he can't speak properly. But at home he said tewna to my wife again, and my wife laughed herself silly too. Stew, she said, st-st-stew.

Oh, the whole neighborhood went back to school with their children that afternoon, even Vieze was there carrying a white bowl in his blue-tattooed hands: 'cause I won't work in Germany, he said. And that said it all: that he was hungry and that they'd have to excuse him if he helped his children out a little with their stew. But to tell the truth, Vieze had never worked, not in Germany and not in Belgium either, and he probably never would, he preferred to beg. But nowadays what he was able to get from the farmers (who were mostly pro-German, he said) wasn't much to brag about—and certainly never stew, he said, watching the school gate eagerly and putting his bowl first under this arm and then under the other. Out came the children then holding their cups in front of them, but it really was tewna, t-t-tewna, after all. Vieze looked at it and said: Jesus, I hate that kind of fish.

WHO GIVES A SHIT ABOUT THE FATHERLAND *even if the whole world now seems full of Belgian patriotism? I'm someone who just wants a bit of food on his table and some coal in his stove, someone who just wants the warmth of his bed and the body of his wife and the eyes of his child, who doesn't feel like the world revolves around him but like a man among men, who loves people* AND NOT FATHERLANDS.

And anyway I've got nothing in common with Adrianus Aesthete, which is just André Asslicker's pseudonym—he's an intellectual and writes in verse, imagine that, and wonders whether he should call what he does "writing," maybe it should be called "giving birth" instead? And who's nearsighted and just goes on giving birth to his verses, giving birth to verses about the moon and about his solitude and about God—and meanwhile is drawing up a list of all the Jewish and communist writers who need to be shot.

A Sentimental Inspector

I'm sitting on our garden bench and since none of the gardens in the neighborhood are fenced off I see a strange gentleman sitting on Staf Spies's garden bench, and he strikes up a conversation with me and says that it's lovely weather for this time of year. And I wonder: who's this? Because when a person wants to talk to you about good or bad weather in the evening you know it's because they've just finished an honest day's work, but when it's still only the afternoon you've usually got someone worth opening your notebook for: men who steal coal at night or smugglers or landscape painters or people from the Black Brigade—who haven't gotten around to causing any trouble today yet, or anyway not in this neighborhood, but who'll be heading off soon to have their fun somewhere else, as they themselves are happy to tell you. And so it turns out that this gentleman is from the meat inspection board, with a face like a beaten dog framed by his bowler hat and grubby collar. He started out in cars, he said, buying and selling, and went bankrupt and so moved into sausages and cheese with someone who knew about sausages and cheese but had no money to get started with—and when he did have money he drank it all up—and then they went bankrupt together. Now he isn't in anything himself and works for the meat inspection board and is sitting there on the bench in the sun. And he tells me story after story, all adventures in which he was the hero and stood up to someone who didn't know what an important man he was dealing with: of course it's possible to make piles of money, he says, I've been in business day and night, though not like What's-his-name, the other guy from the meat inspection board—he goes round to see some farmers supposedly because he's been instructed to inspect their animal sheds and simply says: your stalls aren't up to code, I should report you, I'll be back in 3 days or so. And then he goes back, and nothing's changed in the sheds, except for the fact that there's a ham hanging on the wall for him . . . And at the next farm there are eggs and butter waiting, and at the farm after that there's wheat in a bag or some milk.

Yes, he says to me, you should write a book about that, but they wouldn't believe it . . . I don't know what you write about, I haven't read it, but the things that Ernest Timmermans writes, they rock people to sleep—what a book should really do is wake them up—if I were to write a book, I'd write about that other guy from the meat inspection board. The other day he had a run-in with a wagoner—a real brawl—and then later on he caught this same wagoner going down the street with a lame horse . . . so he chases after him, and there in the street, which I would name if it were of any importance, he sees that the horse is about to keel over.

The guy: your horse is lame.

The wagoner: and what's it to you?

The guy: you can't drive down the street in a cart with a lame horse, look, it's bleeding, and on top of that the thing is completely worn out.

The wagoner: my horse will live to be a hundred.

And so the guy said this and the wagoner said that, the two of them on the pavement and the horse limping along literally on its last legs until they reach the wagoner's house and the horse drops dead, I kid you not. And what happens? They agree to butcher the dead horse properly and sell it off a half-kilo a customer . . .

That's what the sentimental gentleman from the meat inspection board tells me. And the next day my wife asks me whether we could buy a bit of smuggled horsemeat . . . that gentleman who was sitting on Staf Spies's garden bench yesterday killed a horse together with a wagoner, and now they're selling it half a kilo at a time.

And Leentje, the young daughter of the owner of the Café Matisse, who has a very delicate child's body but breasts she can barely carry—they're incredible, when she walks round town she pokes everyone's eyes out with the things—is a little drunk when the planes come and everyone else rushes to the cellar, and what's more is lying there passed out and snoring so disgracefully that her father just decides to put her to bed as quickly as possible, and then gets right in beside her for safety's sake—as he explains to his wife, who catches the two of them in bed the following morning.

And a story only recorded here for posterity's sake, as they say, and that I can still hardly bear to set down—skip this bit, please—is the one about Oscar the butcher, who has a wasting disease and lives with Mariette, whose husband is away working in Germany, and who's living with a German woman there in turn, and how Oscar and Mariette are sitting together in Leentje's house, Leentje from Café Matisse, drinking and drinking till the stuff is leaking out of their ears, just sitting and drinking and leaking. And then they're joined by Maria, who was once a nun but renounced the veil and has cancer now—and who, when she's blind drunk, lifts her skirts and shows the men her bleeding tumor.

And this whole putrid mess—unmentionable diseases, endless drinking and whoring—scares me silly, even when I've got my paltry meat ration to look forward to.

And that same evening in the Town Hall there's a talk on art by a great Flemish poet—if I understood it correctly, says a painter, he meant we shouldn't paint any more drunks, just fine stalwart Flemish types.

Letter

Antoon, who really ought to live in Michigan or Connecticut but because of some mistake happens to be living in a suburb near us, wears a stiff collar and a bowler hat—I've seen him sitting down to dinner and I've seen him sitting in an easy chair having a nap, but that bowler never comes off, I think he even wears it in the bath. He's an electrician and repairs radios and has fixed up his car so that it can serve as his van during the week and then, on Sundays, why not, as a bus for his family—since he has seven kids, the oldest of whom is fifteen and the youngest fifteen months. And so he crams all those children plus a big hamper plus his wife—who's my wife's sister—into that little car and shimmies off into the countryside where he always takes eight 6x9 snapshots with a Kodak: 1 photo of his wife and children, 1 photo of his wife with just the youngest child, then 1 of all the children together, who pull a sillier stunt each time they're photographed. Paula, the eldest, has a face just like her father's, though without the bowler hat. Miriam, who just turned fourteen, and who always looks at you with an inscrutable smile, strikes movie-star poses, seemingly without being aware of it—she has a good chance of turning into a very pretty girl. And Judith, next in line, has her mother's—and my wife's—laugh. The last 6x9 snap has to be of Antoon himself, and so he seats himself at the wheel of his car and his wife has to position herself with the camera so that the damaged mudguard and the door with the missing handle aren't visible. Naturally half the shots are failures.

Let's change the subject: Antoon has a little movie projector that he uses to project an old Western for his family, though the film is constantly ripping, we're experiencing technical difficulties, and is streaked with long lines—a movie in which the heroes make all the familiar gestures of the silent cinema: a young lady frowns, puts her hand to her brow in thought, and all of Antoon's children exclaim: she's thinking now! But apart from this extravagance, Antoon is as conservative as can be, so much so that he used to tell his children: you aren't allowed to go to your uncle's house because he's an anarchist, but since we're both pro-England now, he's allowed his wife to write a letter to mine:

Dearest sister, because the children and Antoon and I live here next to the railway repair shop, where the trains full of German munitions stop every night, we're nervous and would like to move but where can we go with all these children and Antoon's business to worry about? Only yesterday he sold two radios. Every evening we get ready to leave the moment the air-raid warning sounds. Antoon's put together a knapsack for each of us, with our names on them, and we haul them onto our backs the second we hear the siren go, heading out into the street, our youngest has the smallest pack and I have the biggest. And as you've already heard, there's been some bombing here, there was an air-raid warning and the red flares came down and the antiaircraft guns started firing on all sides and the searchlight beams crossed and the bombs fell. We got our bags and Antoon put the baby with the little knapsack on top of his own knapsack and then put his bowler hat over the baby so that it wouldn't see anything—and he said "off we go" and we walked for an hour without stopping, as far as a ditch where Judith finally couldn't go any farther, and neither could I, and where we collapsed on the ground. And while we were lying there I counted the children and there was one missing, the little one, and I said: Antoon, where's our Patrick? And we heard splashing and looked at the stream by the ditch and there was Patrick, still with Antoon's bowler over his head, who couldn't see where he was going, and walked right into the water. Your sister, Emma.

And speaking of people married to Germans: there's a German woman with her husband in line at a movie theater and she's wearing a fur coat—and someone watching her bitterly with greed in his eyes says: God only knows what she'd have to cover her filthy body with back in Germany.

And Italy has capitulated, it won't be long now—it always comes down to that: they've captured What's-it and it won't be long now, the Russians have begun their winter offensive and it won't be long now, and the Finns this and the Turks that and it won't be long now—and soon we'll all be dead and then of course it really won't be long, it'll all be over there and then.

Gas Tank

One evening when we'd been standing at Lazy Corner babbling on and on and had completely solved all the problems of the war and set up a second front and totally annihilated the Germans in Russia because of the cold, Mon from the viscose factory said he'd rather drop dead than lift a finger to help a German. And Emiel who had TB countered that those German boys didn't really have a choice, however you looked at it, though obviously they didn't see things quite the same way we did, since we're for the king and they're for Hitler. And someone else chimed in: we're no more for the king than for anyone else, we're for ourselves and don't want anything except to be left in peace.

So that evening I just sat there watching the falling dusk and saying to myself that each time I saw the sun sink from view behind those demolished houses it got more beautiful, and also wondering how long, how long this war would last, and whether I'd been put on this earth just to witness one after another, the 1st one had barely been over when my father was already saying "you'll be heading off to war again soon" if I happened not to feel like eating lunch, and then after that I was a soldier and after that they were already fighting in Spain, no, the world never seems to recover from this madness. I wasn't sure whether it was the poor simple folk's fault or international finance or because there were too many people or too much was being produced, or whether it was just the earth itself that was sick, a case of the DTs. I was brooding to myself and forgot to respond when Emiel asked me something, and suddenly the planes were there without my having seen them coming. They're German, stay where you are. Sure, but is that one there German too? It's English for Christ's sake, it's a dogfight, run for it! A minute ago we'd just been wasting time on Lazy Corner but now we were in the middle of the war, just like in the theater where you're in a room in Act One and immediately after Act Two plops you in a forest. Somewhere a woman started crying, not because she'd been hit but because she'd lost her head, she was so terrified of dying. All the rest stood and watched. And Padakker who's a hoarder and a nit-picker and likes to be sure of every little thing was half-standing half-kneeling, ready to rush into the cardboard public shelter, "in case anything happens." And all of a sudden something came down, look look, a plane is crashing. And the lower it came, the more clearly we could see it was actually a bomb: it's a bomb it's a bomb! And everyone ran and no one knew where they were running to, and in their rush people scooped up children and then dropped them again because it wasn't "their" child. And all the women were crying and all the children were crying and Lazy Corner was suddenly deserted. And meanwhile, if it had been a bomb . . . But oh, it's too stupid for words, but the thing came spiraling down and it turned out to just be a gas tank. Ha ha, how they laughed and slapped their thighs and wiped the tears from their eyes: they're bombing us with gas tanks now! What a scream: and Staf Spies appeared holding some butcher's paper and shouted: they say they're dropping beefsteaks for us, but I can't find any meat.

And there's Jan Smit who's hard of hearing and stands there cursing about all the bombs BOMBS BOMBS BOMBS—let them blow me to smithereens, but let them get it over with—but who as he crosses the road just in front of a military vehicle gets punched in the face by a German and stands there half dead from fright and looks for a hole in the cobbles to crawl into.

And there's Piet who's joined the blackshirts because he can't make ends meet anymore (and all the people who are earning a pretty penny from the Germans refuse to speak to him) but who can't risk going to Brussels now because he's heard that all the blackshirts are being sent to the Eastern front, so he starts smuggling butter in his uniform—though there's no point, since his wife squanders the money on her lovers anyway, while her kids sleep in the street covered in scabs and lice without so much as a shirt to cover their skinny little asses with.

And Lou who sells shoes that he's stolen from work to someone who sells him coal that he's stolen from the railway—but whenever they see the slightest thing wrong with the merchandise they start screaming at the top of their lungs: goddamn THIEVING BASTARD.

The Two Blind Men

Between my garden gate, frozen shut, and the marshaling yard where the dead trains are parked, along the stretch of water where the dead boats are moored with crewmen still leaning out over their railings, past the factories round the back which always stink, war or no war—it's a mystery how any of the blankets or glucose they make ever comes out smelling okay—all the way to the front door of the hospital: it's all stiff and dead because it's the winter of Stalingrad. Outside the door of the hospital, frozen shut, people stand stamping their feet and pressing their hands over their ears, and it's pointless saying it's cold, since everyone knows it's cold—but come on, what else is there for one person to say to another? And among the people waiting are the two blind men: the peak of one of their caps, the one who's left-handed, is askew, like this, to the left; the peak of the other one's cap, the one who's right-handed, is also askew, like this, to the right—as if they'd each put their hats on correctly at first but then just had to give them one more lopsided tug, to get things perfect. The blind man on the right's overcoat hangs open and is gathered up into a point behind his neck from hanging up on a coatrack too long, since naturally a blind person thinks twice before heading out when it's the winter of Stalingrad and so leaves his coat on the coatrack. And the blind man on the left who has no overcoat, his jacket hangs open and is also sticking up in a point by his neck, with its last button stuck into its second-to-last buttonhole. And they tell a woman who's only letting her red nose peep out from behind her black scarf and who listens to them with one ear while the other is cocked towards the door of the hospital, which still hasn't thawed, about the war and the Volga and the Red October factory. And the woman asks if the war is going to end soon and if any coal is going to arrive and what about milk (and everyone sees—apart from the blind men—that "soon" means: before her little girl is cured, who's in Ward III with TB of the throat). But the war is going to go on for a long time yet, because of this and because of that. And the blind man on the right, calculating, holds up all five fingers of his right hand, while his left hand is still holding the white stick that makes a long sixth finger pointing at the ground.

Then the front door of the hospital finally thaws out at 2 o'clock on the dot, and from the shuffling of the feet passing him and the warmth coming out of the hallway, the blind man on the left realizes that people are going in, first the woman with the red nose, who leaves the blind men and hurries off to Ward III, then the other people hurrying off to the other wards, the ones for men on one side and the ones for women on the other. Come on says the quiet blind man and tugs at the sleeve of the blind man who's still summing up and telling stories and perhaps is about to say "just think of everything we're going to have to go through" to the woman who's been gone now for ages. They point their sticks forward, hold their heads back, lift up their feet, and go in. As for myself, right behind them, I hear the doorman say, "the last ones in should close the door," and so one of the blind men turns round and shuts it in my face. So there I am, outside, between the front door of the hospital, again frozen shut, and the stinking factories and the stretch of water and the back gate of my garden, in the winter of Stalingrad.

And then those Jewish kids who were picked up for no reason on their way back from school and shoved into a truck and taken to the station where they were loaded into a cattle train, and where's the train going?

And someone says those trainloads of Jews are gassed, but I can't let myself believe that if I'm going to keep my conscience quiet, since if a book was going to be written about the war, who'd have the nerve to describe a train like that?

Maybe imagine a movie, you see the train pulling away, but alongside the tracks, among the cinders and the yellow broom, there's a schoolbag lying open, with a penholder and eraser that have fallen out.

And speaking of train tracks, they said on the radio that we should be avoiding them, but how can you avoid train tracks in Belgium?

Try it, go out and walk left or right down the main road, head into the fields, turn your back to the repair shop, and just count the unmanned railway crossings—ha!

And then there are the people who aren't afraid of the planes themselves but of the air-raid siren, and since nine times out of ten the all-clear sounds before the planes have actually left, they all go calmly to bed as though it's the siren that drops the bombs.

And there's that train all ready to depart, parked next to the blank wall of the station—I don't know if you've ever been there, but if you happen to be in the neighborhood, drop by—yes, all ready to go, and suddenly the planes are there and no one can run away, and the whole train and everything in it gets smashed against the wall, so that—Maurice said—they have to be scraped off with spoons.

And then the guy who comes up to you afterward and says, quite indignant: it's a lie, ONLY ten people died.

And the head of Children's Welfare who sells the biscuits and milk he gets for the children of the poor at an enormous profit, which is going too far—imagine!—so that even his cronies say: he shouldn't have done that. And to get rid of him they appoint him editor-in-chief of a German paper in which he writes a series of articles about all these immoral smugglers, under the title: Whatever happened to Christian charity?

That Children's Welfare guy is pro-German, but then there's Horseleg who's a smuggler too and gets drunk every night with a whole bunch of women (oh, I've written this before, unless my memory deceives me, but when a person writes so much it's impossible to remember everything. And apart from that, some things are worth saying twice, since there are plenty of things that can only be half-said each time) and he's pro-Belgium, so who are you supposed to sympathize with? In the long run I guess it's like my wife says: this household's the only real fatherland you've got.

And there are only two kinds of people now, the ones who dig air-raid shelters in the middle of their gardens and the ones who watch and snigger—but then the diggers in turn can be divided into two groups: those who actually take cover in their shelters when the air-raid siren sounds, and those who watch and snigger.

And you hear all sorts of talk about shelters: you can't beat a shelter, I've seen people stuck in a cellar that filled up with shit and I heard about these other people who drowned in their cellar and then there were the ones who suffocated because of a gas leak in a cellar, I wouldn't WANT to be in a cellar, give me a shelter every time.

And in the silence of the night or of the morning or the afternoon, a woman shouting: CAN YOU HEAR THEM!

And the Germans rob you and then the Black Brigade and then the Belgians and then . . . you're forced to rob someone yourself—ashamed at heart.

And you should see the kids from the housing project blocks walking along with swollen knees between their skinny legs and asses. And they've already got bad nerves, children of twelve and thirteen, they've got TB or poor eyesight or stomach cramps that make them writhe with pain. You can hardly go into a house where someone doesn't wet the bed every night.

And in a home like that, the home of someone who's been driven by poverty to work in Germany, who says THINGS ARE GOOD IN GERMANY, *the women wear silk stockings and there's chocolate to eat and there's medical insurance—people like that should have their heads cut off, then you could tell them: take a good look, this is the head of an ass!*

Jean from Tervueren

We're talking about this and that and then someone starts in about the old days of mobilization, and you remember how a German ship was sunk early on with a cargo of shoes . . . and as a result you remember Jean from Tervueren, who laughed himself silly when you used to say that there was going to be war here too: the Germans will never make it, they have no shoes, all we have to do is litter the border with nails. Because you remember you laughed at lots of things in those days which, looking back, are no laughing matter—for example the trenches that hadn't been dug along the border because farmers needed to pass by in their carts.

And then there was Jean himself . . . he was still a kid when the 1914 war broke out and his Dad was killed, so Jean never knew him. And now Jean was expecting a child of his own when he went off to war . . . No, there's never any need to cook up any fantasy, the truth is fantastic enough. And the truth is that you don't even know what happened to Jean from Tervueren. The storm swept over us little Belgian soldiers, and then each of us felt for his own arms and legs, and only later got around to wondering what had happened to such and such. And you never saw Jean again, neither on the Albert Canal nor in the POW camp, and so maybe he's been shoved in the ground with his rifle still in his hand—or maybe he got home like you and me, though why you and me and not others? But apart from that, you remember that he used to talk about Tervueren a lot: he told you 20 times at least how he was allowed to carry the king's clubs once when his majesty played golf there, but only once that he'd been a cabinet maker before the war. And because he saw you filling one sketchbook after another with scribbles, he told you that he'd once done some woodwork for a painter in Tervueren who was world famous, and . . . And once you asked who that painter was, and it turned out to be Edgard Tijtgat of all people. And you exclaimed: I know him, he's got long gray hair and has a pink bump on his nose, and he's always going out to watch the horse-driven mill with his palette in his hand!

But as for Jean himself . . . You'll look him up some day, you think, although you have no idea where he lives in Tervueren, you could go there and ask for the Jean who as a boy went out golfing with the king 20 times—sorry, I mean once—and who may have moved, and who may be long dead. And besides, you say that you'll look him up, but you never do. And that's the saddest thing in life—the saddest thing, that is, when there are no planes around . . . when the red flares aren't floating up there and the air-raid siren hasn't sounded and the bombs aren't falling and you aren't standing there feeling a tightness round your heart, nerves frayed, waiting till the toilet's free—yes, when the planes are gone the saddest thing in your life is that you've known so many people in your life that you'll never see or hear from again.

And who, in a little while, talking about this and that, you won't even be able to remember.

And there's no bread anywhere. The inspectors raided the baker's and the baker escaped by the back door with his smuggled flour, and what's more assures us that on the other side of town every-one's already walking round in tears because they can't get his bread, they've got no bread, no bread and no potatoes, what's to become of us?—and when the inspectors are gone the people all line up again for a smuggled sixty-franc loaf. What else are you supposed to do while you've still got a penny in your pocket?

And Liesje, the daughter of a social democrat but with communist sympathies, believed that the war wouldn't last 3 days before we'd re-ally see something special, rebellion and revolution on all sides—but the war's lasted 4 years now not 4 days and there's still no sign.

And the women huddle in bunches and say "what are we going to do now?" looking at one another—and then they say they'll march behind the black flag, yes, that's what they SAY.

And someone had two cakes baked—guess how much it cost? 700 francs.

Life of Flor

Flor sits down beside me, bums a cigarette, and tells his story . . .

Escaped to France in the last war, Dad in the army, Mom died on the run in France with a note in her hand, she'd written down the address of a cousin in London for myself and my brother, who was two years older. In the confusion lost sight of my brother. Got onto the boat and arrived in London, felt for the note and realized my brother had it, I was 16. Slept on a park bench and met a woman who couldn't understand Flemish and of course I didn't know any English, you can imagine how that went, she sent me out during the day to sell newspapers. You should have seen me standing there, "little Flor with a whole stack of papers in one arm and 1 paper in the other, shouting *daily worker!*" and at night she took me into her filthy bed, which was still better than that bench. Then I suddenly saw a woman from our neighborhood, and called out to her and followed her: Marie! Marie! And Marie said: hey, little Flor! And she took me to a hotel where she washed dishes in the kitchen and where I was able to wash dishes too, you should have seen it, whole chunks of chicken came back and we were supposed to scrape them into the garbage bin, but I scraped them into a bag instead and took it back to Marie's place in the evening and we'd lay there nice and comfortable in bed and eat. Until I was 18 and had to join the Belgian army there in London, and was taken by boat to Westkapelle or Oostrozebeke, let's say Oostrozebeke. And I was going to the front for the first time surrounded by nothing but battle-hardened veterans who'd all been on leave and immediately BOOM what was that? And they laughed at little Flor: oh don't worry, that was a long way off! And we got closer and I saw all those ditches and asked: what's that? That's a communication trench, and my heart pounded and pounded, and we got even closer and boom and boom and boomboomboom and ratatat and bang-bang. Oh and I grabbed the seat of my pants and wanted to hide in a corner and cry, but let myself be pushed onward by our commanding officer who was a good guy and took pity on me and ordered me to take round the brandy ration in the trenches. And I sat down in some out-of-the-way place and drank down the whole bottle and fell asleep and let the others attack, some farm that had to be captured. And then got word from my brother who was also a soldier but was on leave and had actually found that cousin of ours—not in London, as I remembered the note saying, but in Manchester . . . Because you know how it is, you hear about a city in England and you assume it's London. And then I got leave too and went to Manchester, but couldn't stand it with my brother and my cousin and got to know a girl who lived nearby in a tall new block of apartment buildings, and who drank whisky, she and her father and her mother, one whisky after another. And her father said: hurry up, Flor, it's almost seven and you're not drunk yet. Because the pub closed at seven. And then I took them home, her drunk father on one side of me and her drunk mother on the other, and pushed them up that high staircase, and the girl herself following along behind us with her hat all crooked, singing. And I got back home after the war and went into the shoe business and had a shoe factory but my wife got sick so I had to sell my shoe factory and become a traveling salesman, also in shoes. And now war again and day in day out on the streetcar or the train or my bike, always hiding my briefcase so they won't catch me and pack me off to Germany, but luckily I haven't been stopped even once so far. And Flor throws away his cigarette butt, waiting and watching for the rest of your pack.

Oh and people can be divided into two camps again, for instance Fikke who tells us with a gleam in his eye that the Germans are already in Kharkov, and then my father and I who have to admit he's right, but sick at heart—and who wish we could say something back, like . . . well, what could we say that wouldn't be futile, and anyway, if we open our mouths, the Gestapo would be here within the hour.

And there's Kuyle who eavesdrops on people from down in the cellar and then tells the German military police what he's heard—and his wife who's so pro-German that she goes to the movies with all the Germans and lets herself be groped in the dark, and who works for Winter Aid and sells bacon and beans on the side and is earning a fortune—while doctors have had to prohibit children from eating Winter Aid soup, because it makes them wet the bed.

And the parents say: when the war's over the English will bring us white bread and chocolate. And the children ask: what's chocolate?

And there's been an assassination attempt on Hitler and there's a revolution going on and they're already fighting in the streets of Hamburg and Berlin and Kiel, the sailors are destroying their own weapons and the army is fighting against the S.S.—there's been a revolution just like in 1914–18 and the war is over.

And it's not true, Hitler isn't dead and there isn't a revolution just like in 1914–18 and the war isn't over—the Germans commandeer all the remaining cars and the first V-1 flies overhead.

And everyone's tuned to England so eagerly even though there's usually nothing to hear except a call sign—though they even manage to read things into that, it's unbelievable—like Ms. Teresa from the farm, who in the old days only knew about the radio from hearsay and had cow shit on her legs, but who now wears silk stockings, she's bought herself a radio too, and when Churchill says "tomorrow" will be decisive, she rushes round everywhere shouting: they're coming tomorrow! Churchill said so! And everyone locks their doors and huddles down in their cellars.

Simple Story

This is a story—exactly as it was told to me, without my adding one word to pretty it up or leaving out one word that might give offense—from Gaston who was arrested and thrown in the Blackout Cell, chained hand and foot for eight days (when it rains you can still see the welts) and unable to relieve himself. And on the ninth day he couldn't hold it in any longer and pissed himself and then he was pushed into his own piss. And the same guy that had arrested him interrogated him, and he said he didn't know anything, that he'd just found a note in his mailbox—and so they took something he didn't know what to make of out of a cupboard and slapped him across the face with it. At first he didn't notice anything, it didn't even hurt, but a few seconds later it all became clear: it was a rubber-covered cloth that stretched and shrank when it hit you so the skin got torn right off your face. And then he was thrown into solitary and every day he had to go back for a dose of the rubber cloth, so that eventually when he was on his way down the hall he started thinking: oh I wish I were safe in my cell. And then they threatened to send him to their torture chambers if he didn't talk—ha, and he told them some bullshit and they actually believed it, for Christ's sake. And eventually he was able to talk to someone from another cell, down the central heating pipe, and he said: I'm Gaston. And the other guy said: I'm André. And he told him his wife's name and what town he came from and how he'd planted tobacco in his back garden, and the other guy said: so did I. And after that he wanted to see André in person, so when they were coming back from the exercise yard he pretended to get confused and went into the wrong cell, just for a second, and said: hi André. And the other guy said: hi Gaston. And he was happy.

And then he was transferred to another prison where there were three cells on top of each other (and I nodded, because Josie had told me about that too), and sometimes, about four times in all, someone just threw himself right over the railing from the top cell. And Sunday afternoons the prisoners would smash the glass in their cells' one-way peepholes so that they could take a look at everyone going by, and they all got to know each other by sight. And there was an electrical socket they'd removed so that they could talk to each other through the recess, but the guards had caught him red-handed and knocked his teeth out with a wrench, so he had to swallow his food unchewed, and it stuck in his stomach in a ball, which made him writhe in agony. Oh but that was nothing, they'd beaten another guy all over his chest with the rubber cloth and then sent him home even though he'd been sentenced to death—and it would have been better if they'd shot him, at least then he would have been able to shout Long Live Belgium and would have died a hero and his wife would have been able to draw a pension, but instead he had to sit there at home dying in a chair and his family had to spend their last few pennies on him and what else can you expect from the government, really? And then Gaston had to go to Merksplas where it was quite nice because he was allowed to get packages, but afterward he had to go to the French coast to carry bags of cement, wearing clogs—and when the clogs were worn out wearing socks, and then in his bare feet. When they first arrived there were jackets and pants hanging from the trees, because of the bombing raids, you can imagine the impression that made. It was hell, really hell. And he counted the days till the end of his sentence and told himself every night that there were only X number of nights left for them to bomb him, and then bombs fell in the latrine and the whole camp was covered in shit. And then his sentence was over but he wasn't released, the Wehrmacht said that as far as they were concerned he didn't have to stay in jail, but Organisation Todt was in charge there and they had nothing to do with the Wehrmacht. His wife went everywhere trying to get him out, even to see a senior German officer sitting in his office in the nicest house in town, he was just being served drip-brewed coffee and there was a German whore sitting on his lap with her legs between his and they made Gaston's wife stand there like a beggar woman. And finally he just made a break for it, some night when there was yet another raid and everyone was running round like a lunatic, and he snuck on and off trains without a permit or papers or anything, and was unbelievably lucky.

And now he has to keep out of sight, but do you think anyone really cares about him? Now we eat jam sandwiches and sleep all day—that makes you fat.

And they found a German soldier in the corn off the country lane I always go down to see Gaston—some children heard him screaming, just like a wild animal. And I'd been by just five minutes earlier but again didn't hear or see anything. And they carried him out of the corn, which wasn't ripe yet—he hadn't eaten for seven days and the only sounds his swollen throat could produce were animal noises. He had really thick legs and feet that had been torn to shreds and were covered in congealed blood, and he was given milk to drink—he was given milk and white bread and the children from the apartment blocks, who had forgotten the taste of white bread, watched wide-eyed. He said that he'd run away from the coast, that he'd deserted, and they asked him where he wanted to hide and he said: military police headquarters. Pierre thinks he's headed for the firing squad.

And Gaston says deserters are sent up a tall hill to push stones down from the top that they then have to retrieve, carry up, and then push down again.

And Gust the hairdresser says no they won't shoot a deserter if he's not 21: in Germany you're allowed to get a girl pregnant at 15 but you don't count as a full soldier till you're 21.

And Karel the butcher says: tut-tut, he's a soldier and all soldiers have to go out to the front to meet Old Nick.

Oh how wonderful popular expressions can be: a plane that's been hit and comes limping home an hour after the other planes is a plane ON CRUTCHES.

Piano for Sale

We could sell our piano, said my wife, and I didn't say anything and wouldn't look her in the eye because I knew what the piano meant to her: it was the only thing left we could point to, the last remaining evidence of our middle-class status. And also, why hide it, I knew what the piano meant to me too: I liked sitting on the bench in our garden and listening to the piano-sounds coming from the house, even if it was only someone playing *drops of rain beat at your window pane*. Because some people like a glass of beer and other people like to watch the girls riding by on their bikes, but I like the evening and the tinkling sounds of a piano—oh what idiotic romanticism, but futile to resist it. And I made a sign saying "piano for sale" for us to put in the window and we felt like spiders waiting for a fly. I said: I think the sign's too small. And the baker came by, and we tried to pay him off quickly so as to start work on a bigger sign, but he just stood there with his long stupid face. That piano, he said, can I have a look? We showed it to him and stood and watched him expectantly. Well, you couldn't tell much from his face, it looked as idiotic as usual. No, he said finally, I thought it was one of those things that plays by itself. They've got a piano that plays itself when you put in a quarter at the bar round the corner, maybe they'll sell that to you, my wife suggested. We all went to see the electric piano, the baker had to laugh when he saw the keys going up and down without anyone lifting a finger, it's like magic, he said. He didn't ask the price, he was just worried about how he'd get it home. We'll shove it in the cart and I'll hitch up my horse, said the owner of the bar, but first I'll buy a round. The baker wouldn't let him. I'll buy a round. So they both bought a round, and then the baker bought another and the owner another and finally we all stood there looking bleary-eyed at the piano with its keys still going up and down *Ramona when day is done you'll hear me call* and the baker knew the tune and sang along, he danced with the owner's wife and he bought another round. He remembered his father who'd been a desperately poor baker before the war, then got killed in the air raids, and remembering his father he started crying, crying because he can't see the money I'm making now, the baker said. The bar door opened and the baker's wife came to see where he'd got to. I suppose you're drinking 35-franc shots again, she said. He pulled her inside and held her tight and danced with her. He wanted her to have a drop too. He cried and said: I was just telling them how it's so terrible that my father can't see the piles of money we're making. Be quiet, said his wife. And the piano stopped and we all went quiet. The baker looked at us with his stupid face and stood up straight and tried to show he wasn't drunk, I know exactly what I'm saying. You don't know what you're saying at all, his wife replied. And she said that nowadays everyone thinks bakers are making a fortune profiteering, but it's not true: anyway, after the war people will realize how much the bakers have done for them. How's that? asked the owner. And he also asked why it was that the ration bread was so bad, I don't think there's a scrap of flour in it. Of course there's no flour in it, just bran and rolled oats and ground chestnuts. Still, said the owner, if you buy ration flour and bake your own bread there's flour in it, so what's going on? And the baker with the stupid face said nothing, he walked out and his wife followed him, and they came and bought OUR piano after all, the one they had to play themselves even though they can't play, neither the baker nor his wife. But I'll make sure little Mies plays it, he said.

And when the planes are overhead the rich people who are pro-Belgium say: why do they have to DROP BOMBS DROP BOMBS every night—but they keep their gates locked so that the workers trying to flee the factories or the train station don't run through their gardens and trample the grass.

And the poor people who blame the rich people for that—very quietly, so they don't hear—ask: is that being pro-Belgium? But when they steal coal from the railroad, they sell it to the rich people and sit in the cold.

And the ones who are pro-England won't hear a word said against the English, they're good and brave and the best soldiers and they can swing dance and swing dancing is the best kind of dancing there is—while the others say the English are cowards who can't do much besides dance, and swing dancing is the most indecent kind of dance there is.

And the Gestapo raid the house and push my wife into a corner and come running into my garden just as I'm trying to push some lopsided sprouts into the soil—it's only to check my papers but I thought it was the end of me, I could already feel the rubber cloth on my face.

And then there are the kids who dream up a new fashion as the bombs rain down, let their hair grow long and wear pants that are too short—and also the S.S. men who raid a dance hall guns in hand just to scare the shit out of the wartime kids.

 And only yesterday the S.S. raided a house and beat the wife and raped the kids and smashed up their last few sticks of furniture. Afterward it turned out they'd got the wrong address.

And there's Bral who confesses to me that he wept at the fall of Stalingrad: now the Bolsheviks will be coming, he said, his asshole squeezed tight with fear.

And Boone's daughter says that the Russians have bombed Berlin, because Bolsheviks aren't human—but what about the Germans wiping out Russian towns? I can't believe that, she says.

Albertine Spaens

Albertine Spaens was a very good and very amusing and very ugly person, who had to have all her teeth pulled out because they'd all come loose thanks to malnutrition, and who had no money to have any new ones put in and so simply walked around with the eyes of a thirty-year-old and the mouth of an eighty-year-old. Every lunchtime she went with us to the Leopold III soup kitchen, where they'd scrape two potatoes and a piece of meat into a bowl for us (shut the door quickly, so it doesn't all blow away). What's-her-name came too, what *was* her name again, the one who was hit in the head with something the other day and died, who used to get so furious and denounce us as pro-German when we said the war would last five years, "that's impossible, because my husband was counting on a blitzkrieg, and if it lasts more than another month I don't know what we're supposed to do"—and who aside from that was always coming out with the oddest things imaginable and even said Lode Zielens was a bad writer . . . it was Mrs. Lammens! And Albertine Spaens used to laugh at all of Mrs. Lammens's ridiculous assertions—she used to laugh at everything, for that matter . . . at the Winter Aid soup and the people in line and the Germans' posters . . . And yes, I remember too that on our way back we sometimes bumped into a pro-German primary school teacher we wouldn't talk to anymore, even though he was a nice enough guy with a bowler hat and big splayed feet. Despite everything he continued to say good day very politely: good day Mrs. Lammens, good day Mrs. Spaens. And Albertine, who'd been laughing herself silly the whole way, turned to him once and said, reluctantly: good day. And then, once: I'm losing all my teeth from hunger. And the next day: it always hurts, and here too . . . and she put her hand on her heart . . . but apart from that she went on laughing and keeping our spirits up and saying: folks, one day the war really will be over and those gray lice will all be crushed, and then we'll learn how to swing with our old legs, although I'm afraid there'll be two Albertine Spaenses by then, I already feel like I'm splitting in two. And she pushed at her heart again, she pushed at it more and more, sometimes she stopped on a street corner with her can of soup in her hand and called after us: hold on a second, wait for me! And finally she asked: could you carry my soup for a bit?

And then one day I met her on her way to a heart specialist. I'd just seen the streetcar pull out when she came chasing round the corner panting and gasping for breath with her toothless mouth. She was trying to ask if the streetcar had already left, but she couldn't manage, she slumped against a wall and eventually asked if I would take her home. Oh, and a blackshirt came by with his clumping boots and forced her to lift her head up and stop loitering. And then her heart trouble turned out to be advanced cancer which simply had to be removed. She went into the hospital, but four years of hunger had taken too great a toll, and she never made it home again, she was lying there dying the very same day that our friends from across the channel came to pay Belgium a visit. And Mrs. Berens and Mrs. Lammens—who's also dead now—and I all stood round her deathbed and bent over her and said: they've landed! And she raised her head for a moment and looked at us and said: ha, then drape a Belgian flag over my orange crate, and by evening she was dead.

And then there's What's-his-name who's taken up with the black-shirts and who throws his wife out onto the street in her petticoats whenever he comes home drunk out of his mind and who buys everyone who'll say Heil Hitler a drink and goes to nightclubs and blows 50,000 francs in a single evening—because he's been promoted from small-time carpenter to big boss of local wood distribution.

And my parents say it's a blitzkrieg, it won't last long—and for that matter it CAN'T *last much longer, we've already had to borrow money on our house—and since I have to disappoint them and say that it* will *last a while, I'm denounced as pro-German.*

And the people ask the pastor if instead of going to church they can pray in the chapel, which is closer to home—but the pastor, who's likely to end up with no one left in his congregation, says no: what's the difference, he asks, or do you really think that the planes will drop less bombs just because you're praying a little closer to home? And the people say: if we're not allowed to use the chapel we'll just pray outside in the street. And I'll forbid you to, says the pastor, I'll have you all chased away.

And the decline of public morals is increasing so alarmingly, an old whore wonders what the world is coming to: in my day . . .

And the children follow a German soldier and ask if he's back from Normandy. Yes, he says, but we'll be going back again soon with new weapons. And he buys the children an ice cream—one—and the whole gang wants a lick of the ice cream, and he hears them say "lick," which sounds almost the same as it does in German, and so he tells them: everyone lick. And the children ask if he knows Flemish then, and if he knows they're dropping bombs on Germany. And they point out Kuyle's son and say: he's a black-shirt—and just look how proud he is!

The First Hour

For the last few nights we haven't been able to sleep, usually I've lain in an armchair by the open back door with a blanket round my legs, looking at the stars, smoking cigarettes and listening to the distant drone of the planes—going inside occasionally and listening to the call sign of the English radio broadcasts. And just before midnight, tararaboom, I heard the tune they used to play at every opportunity, when their king died or something, but which now after four years still made my heart leap into my mouth: our troops have crossed the Belgian frontier, they announced. My wife, who'd taken over from me smoking cigarettes and keeping an ear out for the planes, came in and stood next to me without closing the back door—how careless, when there are Germans driving by. Is that truck full of wounded still there? I asked. No, it's gone, she said. And I looked at her, she had a gray woolen stocking over her head and my overcoat with the collar up round her shoulders. You look just like a Russian, I said, but she didn't laugh: I could just cry my eyes out, Louis love, I could just cry my eyes out. But she didn't need to say so, she was already doing it. And we made coffee quick as we could and went out to listen to the grapevine on the street. They're there! said my wife, and sure enough we could hear them advancing in their hobnail boots, we threw open the front door and at the same moment we heard, very faintly, since the wind was blowing the wrong way, the carillon ringing. And what was that? Sounded like cheering. And in the meantime too there were men already marching down our street—there was too much to see and hear all of a sudden—but these were still Germans, marching two abreast right by the houses, so we withdrew deep into the shadows and held our breaths. *Vorwärts*, they shouted. And little Mr. Brys, who used to be a well-to-do bourgeois but had come down in the world since the war, and who picked cigarette butts off the street when no one was looking, opened his window and hung out the tricolor—or so we assumed, since in the dark it was just a black rag. And a bit further on people were smashing all the windows at Charlot the cripple's house, he'd picked up that bum leg of his in the trenches in the last war, then became a blackshirt during this one—where's the sense in that? And then we heard footsteps again, listen I said, and someone was singing the Marseillaise, it was probably Proske and his wife. And What's-his-name, said my wife. Which What's-his-name? I asked . . . the one they'd dragged out of bed a couple of weeks ago before, she'd told me about it herself when it happened, her eyes big as anything, lower lip quivering, looking round to make sure we had everything well-hidden, but what did we have left to hide, what book did we have left to burn? Not a one. *Enfants de la patrie* . . . and it was as though my blood had frozen while my brain was busy bursting into flames, as though I no longer had hands to clench into fists. *Formez vos bataillons* . . . and they marched past in serried ranks and we shivered and cheered them, those boys with hand grenades in their belts. There were only ten of them, but that didn't stop us cheering the 990 other ones out there sitting on the English tanks. We cheered the English and the Americans and the Canadians and the Scots and the boys in the White Brigade—even though I saw several who'd been in the Black Brigade the previous day . . . but at that moment we were color-blind: it was the first hour.

And then English deserters were being dragged out of every hidey-hole you could think of, from Florine and Elise's place, you name it.

But all the poets who wrote so enthusiastically about the Eastern front peeked out cautiously in their socks, back to writing poems about the stars and their solitude and God—God for God's sake—after having pissed right onto Christ's loincloth.

And a man who walks with a stick—they say because he fell out of a moving car—always crosses the street when he sees me coming, because he thinks I'm a poet too. And poets are all fools, he says, what's the difference between a poet and a whore.

And I'm sad that he thinks that—not the bit about poets being like whores, but that I might be a poet.

The Profiteers

On the edge of town, next to the dump that pollutes the whole suburb during the summer, next to the sawmill, lives Mr. Swaem, who runs a shoe factory called "The English Shoe," and who made boots all through the war, at first secretly for Organisation Todt and later shamelessly for the Wehrmacht. They drove up in their trucks while the gate was closed and all the lights were out. Mom, short and fat and with a real mean streak, would go up to the German officers and speak to them in a German that wasn't German but cultured country Flemish with lots of gestures, wearing a grin that, out of stupidity, said: oh, don't mind us earning so many millions from you that we've already been able to afford three pianos, four fur coats and two radios—one for the lounge where all the German officers sit around and get plastered with us and one for upstairs where Dad listens to the

English station to find out what to do with our money. And Dad, who was just as fat and just as mean, and who fought with himself every day to shake off the vestiges of little Swaem the schoolmaster and become the great Mr. Swaem, would walk from one end of his factory to the other puffing ostentatiously on a fat cigar, but still couldn't resist rushing to the gate after every broadcast so he could tell everyone what the English had just said. But apart from Boone, who lived next door and sold tires to the German army and had earned a fortune from it and ate rabbit or chicken every lunchtime and who cursed a blue streak if he was unlucky enough to just get steak and fries—apart from this Boone it was only the poor folk from the suburbs who listened respectfully to Mr. Swaem's reports, but all the time they were thinking: after the war we're going to have you thrown in jail. And all this didn't stop Boone from being an Anglophile who listened to The Voice of America and said that they had these Flying Fortresses that the German planes crashed into and got stuck on, hanging there in pieces, so that the Americans flew back to America with them still dangling there—because those Americans are really tough! And then he stuffed half a bunch of grapes in his mouth, at 400 francs a kilo, so that the juice ran down his chin. And Mr. Swaem said: let them give the Germans hell, because they're all bastards and I know what I'm talking about, I was a POW in the last war. And putting his fat hand to his mouth to show it was secret, yet loud enough to be heard on the far side of the dump, he also said: I gave 10,000 francs to the White Brigade. And suddenly it was the liberation and there on the edge of town it was almost like a fair: there was a flag hanging from the shoe factory that was so big you couldn't see the front of the building except for a bit of the gutter, and there was a banner hanging between the factory and Boone's place reading: WELCOME. And one of the White Brigade's cars pulled up beneath that welcome, and they went into Mr. Swaem's place with guns in their hands, but came out again with cigars between their lips.

And did the people of the suburb have the Swaems thrown in jail? No, it was all a mistake, if you ask them now nobody even remembers anything about German trucks loaded with boots.

And a few women say that the English are bastards too because they shot at them when they went to steal coal as usual on the railways—but they won't tolerate hearing an ex-blackshirt run the English down, because when they insult the English and when the blackshirts insult them it's a VERY DIFFERENT MATTER.

And Louis who's an anarchist, a nihilist, and a dirty old man, says we must all get down on our knees and pray to God to deliver us from the Canadians.

And Philomène who worked in Germany and came back with a kid, a German's of course, now goes out dancing with Canadians while the planes pass overhead on their way to bomb Berlin—and she says: you can't go on mourning FOREVER, can you?

In Praise of the Boswell Sisters

In those awful days, I only had to take one step toward the radio and my wife would say: is this really a time to be listening to music? And I would reply: it's the Boswell Sisters, as if the Boswell Sisters were more than just music. Because this is a hymn of praise to the Boswell Sisters. If I were a great poet I might sing the praises of Bach and Beethoven, who people won't shut up about and in whom they hear the sea and the forests and God Himself, but who just remind me of the sawmill up at Gust Nest. And of course if I were an even greater poet I'd sing the praises of jazz, the soul of our ruined age, of our desperation and rage and despair—of our age in which none of us, individually, feel the least bit at home, but which no other generation but ours could endure, oh Armstrong and your trumpet. But I'm not a great poet, all I can do is say a few things about our street, so I'm only famous in our street, while the Boswell Sisters, they're famous all over the world. And in those miserable days when I went over to the radio to try and brush away the tweettweeting of the interference and listen to you, oh you Boswell Sisters, I was almost grateful to live in this age. I heard your songs through the interference and I can't describe it, I'd have to write down the lyrics and then print tweetweetweet on top of them. And then there was one time the Gestapo came in just when you'd started singing but they somehow didn't notice, they just asked for my papers and left again, and I turned all pale once they were gone and thought: I'll write a novel about this one day. But now I find it so uninteresting that I couldn't even manage to write three lines about it, whereas I could write 300,000 just about you. And then later, when we were breathing easier again and could listen to the Free Dutch station from England, I heard you again without interference, oh you beloved Boswell Sisters, who mean more to me than Bach or Beethoven. And, I should tell you something else, but it's something I don't want anyone to hear . . . so how can I? I'll have to write it in a book you'll never read, but which I still hope you might, somehow . . . who knows . . . Tell you what, I'll write it very fast and then cover it with my hands so that no one but you can read it: I listened to you, and something faraway vibrated in me, and my wife asked: why are your eyes so wet?

And there's the touching case of three old men who are sitting and chatting and one old man asks: what kind of fun is there left for them nowadays? And the other two sit there nodding and for all we know probably thinking he doesn't know what he's talking about.

And I wonder what constitutes "fun" in an old man's head anyway.

The Last One

On Friday afternoon a truck stopped on Stalin Avenue, full of Canadian girls. Certainly I always thought it was stupid of my wife to leave the pot unattended on the stove and stand cheering at the front door whenever Allied soldiers drove past. Yes, but now they're Scotsmen, she said. As if that made any difference, the next day it was African Americans or Native Americans, oh, a soldier's a soldier. But now: there are Canadian girls on Stalin Avenue, I said, and I was already out in the street. They'd jumped out of their trucks and were jabbering and smoking and looking for a café and finding EVERYTHING interesting. After all, they'd come here from faraway Canada precisely to see something interesting, and maybe they all felt it was a little late to be finding out that everything was perfectly ordinary here, rather cold and foggy and sad. And they kept warming their hands on their illusion like it was a campfire. Despite their boots and their uniforms, their permed hair and shiny eyes and lipstick all shouted: we haven't come to defeat Hitler but to see something of the world! And if they'd been like the girls from our neighborhood, they might have had the guts to add: and find a sweetheart! I was grateful to them for that, actually, that they weren't like women in uniform, but like girls. And in the last truck sat the last girl who didn't smoke cigarettes and didn't jabber and didn't pretend—because she'd let the campfire of her illusions go well and truly out, the clumsy thing. I walked past her, she was cold and was probably curling her toes in her boots as she looked out and handed a package to a woman from our street, who immediately tucked it under her shawl and said *merci* in embarrassment. She, this last girl, hadn't come to conquer the world, but to give a package to a woman from Belgium. And as I looked at her, I understood her, so well she might have been my own sister—she had a harelip.

And why or how I don't know but that reminds me of the last German I saw, who might as well have been my brother, he was sitting on an English truck in the drizzling rain, and he looked at me, and with a rather sorry smile he stuck his thumb up—"OK!"—just as he'd seen the English do.

And they ask me to write for a magazine and one of the other contributors reads my piece and says that he'd rather something like that didn't get repeated—certainly, certainly, it's all right if pieces of mine are published now and then, it provides a harmless bit of vulgar, comic relief, but not too often please, people might eventually get the idea that he's THE SAME SORT OF WRITER.

Justice

We always knew Proske as someone who'd rather die than have
to say black when something looked white to him—and we
used to have a lot of good laughs because of the trouble he'd get
himself into. He'd say: *what?* And then he'd straighten up and
turn in his notice or punch the factory manager in the face or
throw his wife out onto the street. Of course he didn't have a
subtle enough intelligence to realize that there might be such a
thing as dark black and pale black. And then the war came, and
the revulsion welled up in him so fiercely that he was even less
able than usual to express his thoughts clearly: he had to pound
them into people. Every Saturday afternoon he'd show up with
some new batch of newsprint, Stalin's latest speech or else the
Dean of Canterbury on the Soviet Union or else Free Belgium
or the Red Star, and once he even tried to start his own paper,

"Moscow–London Calling"—I was commissioned to design the masthead and he explained to me how he wanted it: a fist on one side and on the other two parted fingers and in the middle the star of the League of Nations. I'd draw it myself, he said, but I haven't got the time. But when the design was finished he didn't show up anymore—he forgot about it for the first two weeks and then spent the next two locked in a cell. Oh, but he came back eventually, he was immortal, it was his destiny to cause trouble and even a thousand Gestapo men couldn't stop him from doing that. If they'd bumped him off his ghost would still have come back after the war and reared up in our midst, shouting: *what?*

There he was, marching along on that memorable morning when the Germans finally made a run for it, with a submachine gun under his arm, waving at me and laughing and hopping restlessly from one leg to the other, because the barracks over there on the square would be too small for all the prisoners he was going to collect once he started his great blackshirt cleanup. But he mellowed, he gradually began to find time to drop in again for a few minutes on Saturday afternoons to tell us his troubles. We political prisoners, he said. Just like he used to say: we men of whatever This or That he happened to belong to at the time . . . And there was no justice, no, none none none . . . What's-his-name, he said, you know, the top man at the What's-his-name & What's-his name Factory, they released him so he can emigrate to Switzerland, can you believe that, while the small fries all stay in jail. And it was pointless trying to . . . he interrupted whatever hesitant opening words I was trying to get out with a new complaint that brought a sad kind of tone to his voice, difficult to pin down: and now we've got to surrender our weapons! So on the one hand they're releasing the men I arrested and on the other hand they're taking my weapons away . . . if you happen to come by our neighborhood some night, do me a favor and take a look in any ditches you might pass, make sure I'm not lying in one with a bullet in my belly.

And what actually happened I don't know, because I don't want to know, but Proske's back in jail. Then one day I hear the doorbell and there he is again, now a member of the P.W.W.P.W.P.P—the union of Pre-War, Wartime, and Post-War Political Prisoners.

And listening to those poets on the radio writing about everything under the sun, their art and their inspiration and their heaven knows what—I'd like to hear one of them be interviewed about it all and then answer the first question by saying, poker-faced: sorry, I'm afraid I couldn't tell you the first thing about that stuff, sir.

And Jan who's reading these pages asks me if the comma key on my typewriter is broken—of course not I say—so why do you use so few? he asks.

Someone from Buchenwald

Oh, a terrorist? A terrorist was one of those people who would creep through the streets like an anarchist at night, bomb in hand, pants tattered and hanging round their legs, combing their hair while looking into their reflection in your doorknob. Until the first real terrorist entered my house and I saw he was a gentleman with horn-rimmed glasses and a dark-blue tie with light-red stripes, so that my wife told me later: you should buy yourself a tie like that. And to top it all off he wore patent fucking leather shoes. His said his name was André, but of course that was just his undercover name to throw people off his scent—and at first I thought that he was also trying to throw them off his scent with his clothes, since the way he sat down so carefully to keep the crease in his trousers, he was more like a dandy than a terrorist. Vieze was sitting there too, and told him they should turn Germany into one big crater, and André opened his eyes wide in dismay and said: it would be sad for all those old churches and castles to be destroyed. And when I object that anyway they're just a load of old stones, they could build new churches after the war, he looked at me . . . yes, the same way I'd looked at his patent leather shoes. Afterward I heard that he'd been a museum curator before going underground, or anyway one of those jobs where people fight a hopeless battle with dust. But look, I'll add something that absolutely typifies him: he had to keep up contact with a terrorist based in the harbor district who happened to be a girl, you know—they like to call them all sorts of terrible names just because they're in the Resistance but aren't men—I don't know what the difference is, one's a seamstress and the other a typist and another a whore—and that girl said: oh, André? He's like a close girlfriend.

But André too took that goddamn road to Calvary from Gestapo headquarters to Breendonk and from Breendonk to Buchenwald, and there in Buchenwald they came for him YET AGAIN—and if they came for you there, that was it . . . might as well make the sign of the cross over you. They tied his hands behind his back and took him to the gallows, where . . . oh, I almost said "where his last necktie was waiting for him," but that sounds kind of . . . of . . . especially when you think about how hundreds of our best people went out the same way, with their hands tied behind their backs. But as he stood there ready, the planes suddenly arrived, and the air-raid siren sounded, and they started bombing the S.S. barracks, so that everyone ran away and left André there alone, next to his gallows. And when the planes were gone they all came back out of their hiding places and looked for André, but he was gone, he'd hidden himself among the dead, he'd taken the papers of a dead Frenchman and swapped them for his own papers. André was dead—he'd lived underground over here with us and then over there in Buchenwald he lived illegally for the second time.

And now he's back, he sits down cautiously and asks politely how things are, and when I ask how he managed over there he tells me the thing about Buchenwald that really shook him to the core: I had to do fatigues, but you know what else they made me do? He goes quite red and his head droops in embarrassment, and then he says so quietly he can barely even hear himself: shovel out the latrines.

How the poor little sucker sees it all: oh Christ suddenly you shit yourself and then you're dead anyway.

And then there's the sergeant from the mine-sweeper unit who's sitting in the streetcar with a delicate blonde lady and wowing her by telling her how they go about detonating mines: we lay a cable out to the mines and then trigger them from a shelter: boom. And he makes a gesture with his fist, twisting it round—and the windows get blown out everywhere, haha, BUT SOMETIMES THERE ARE DUDS.

What's a dud?

Well, the ones that don't explode and that we still have to find, and he makes a shape like this with his thumb and fingers: a little heart beating anxiously. And the delicate blonde lady begins to purr with pleasure.

Le Drapeau

We draftees in the Belgian army graciously allowed them to conduct large-scale army maneuvers with us in the Beverloo Camp and so along came a specimen of the prewar officer class asking where the enemy was, and What's-his name looked at this specimen in silence and who just said *idiot* and then moved on. And What's-his-name turned to me and said: how could I tell him that HE was the enemy?

Because who is your enemy, really? Someone who doesn't speak your language properly and calls you an *idiot* and who's paid to give decent food to the soldiers but pockets the money and feeds you with inferior provisions, who makes his soldiers' lives a living hell and who . . . well, in short, is your enemy. And you only really start to realize this once and for all when you see those American officers playing poker with their men in a café—only yesterday I saw a soldier tap his captain on the shoulder and say: hey, would you like a drink? In an army like that it must be fun being a cowboy, I mean soldier.

And that was just by way of an introduction, because I actually want to write about a commander in the Belgian army, he was called Machin or something, I don't remember exactly, but if you meet him in town you'll recognize him right away. One day he was an officer tormenting his soldiers and the next day he was in civvies tormenting his workers in his capacity as his-sister's-brother in his sister's factory. And then the enemy invaded the country and of course he got out, ran as far as his legs would carry him, he almost drove his car right into the Mediterranean. But of course in his capacity as his-sister's-brother he came back as soon as the worst of the onslaught was over, because how was the factory going to make blankets for the German army without him? He came back in his civvies and all he did was smuggle coal: sabotage, he called it (I'd like to know what exactly he sabotaged, apart from the wallets of the poor)—but don't think he went underground or led an attack on a German train or helped print and distribute manifestos. No, on the contrary, he was the one who agreed with the members of the pro-German organizations to allow local coal dealers to transport their coal to Wallonia—supposedly for sale on ration.

And lo and behold, on the first day of the liberation—or no, the second day, because on the first day there was still some fear that the Germans, who were surrounded, might break back out—on the second day of the liberation he appeared in the street again in the uniform of an officer in the Belgian army, drove around with English gasoline, and people were doffing their caps to him as he stood at attention at the gate of the barracks where the blackshirts were being detained. He sat at an enormous desk and wrote reports and spoke French and did absolutely nothing useful—on the contrary, he made a mess of everything and lost files and immediately helped the members of the fascist movement "The Flag" get released. That was the last straw, Proske couldn't stand it anymore, so he confronted him and asked: do you know what kind of organization The Flag was? And Machin or whatever got on his high officer's horse and replied: Ze Flak? *Mais oui c'est Le Drapeau.*

And a lady, still well-dressed but already crumbling, is sitting on the train looking at the pages featuring ads for the "sale of old furniture," and she tears an ad out and then a little further on there's another that she also tears out—and then a little on further there's another that she overlooks, and a worker who's sitting next to her and who was reading along says: Madame, you missed one.

And then there's my son Jo who goes to school in the morning but at lunchtime a boy stops by and says the teacher told him to tell us that my son Jo hasn't been to school. And you should have seen my wife's face: she doesn't know whether she's going to drop dead or what—maybe Jo's been run over or hit by a bomb, maybe he's already in the morgue. And I go looking for him and find out that he simply didn't go to school—because my shoes are hurting me, he says. Because he knows that I CAN'T buy him new shoes.

Letter about Lea Lûbka

Dear friend you may remember Lea Lûbka, the Jewish girl we used to call Liesje during the war, and who'll never have any other name for me because that was her nom de guerre, and who always sat at home knitting so quietly—I don't actually know what she was knitting and she probably had even less idea herself—in the hours when she didn't have any underground newspapers to deliver or didn't have any bags of explosives to carry through town, and who once every couple of weeks would open her mouth and let her thoughts out, so deep and beautiful you could read through the great philosophers and not come up with anything to match her. I painted her once as an "immigrant" sitting there with a bundle on her knees and her child standing in front of her looking right up through the bundle at the next thought ripening inside her, which she might finally let out of her mouth in another couple of weeks. But again, it wasn't right, that painting, like your writing isn't right—try and remember one of those nights when we were still honest and naïve and sat under the iron bridge looking at the reflection of the yellow lights in the black water and said: I shall never paint and never write anything except what's deep and beautiful and true. And now you write jokes and I paint Mickey Mouse designs on fairground tents. But Liesje never spoke that last beautiful thought of hers, unless it was over in Germany, after they deported her there. And then yesterday—I get home and turn the radio on without listening to it as one does and suddenly I hear her name being read out: Lea Lûbka is returning alive and well from the camp at Mauthausen. And I pace round between my four walls and say to the failed painting where she's sitting there looking at her bundle and at the cracked cup that she just drank out of and at the wobbly chair on which she's been sitting knitting something that must have been much bigger than just a pair of socks (maybe she was knitting what we were all longing for in those days, the distant reflection of which I still sometimes try to find in your eyes, fool that I am), yes, I shout at it all: she's coming back she's coming back! And I walk round the streets and say to the sky and the trees in the boulevard and to the people hawking black-market cigarettes (*Anglaises!*): she's coming back! I shout it, scream it, whisper it. And I stop by Piet's place—and Piet's brother is there too, I've saved myself a walk, since I'd been planning to go round to his house too—but then I go ahead and stop by his place anyway, though Leo never knew her all that well, but that's not the point, the point is to say it everywhere. Everywhere. LEA LÛBKA'S COMING BACK.

And then this morning a letter from Sweden saying that Lea Lûbka died out in Germany: we, her friends, did everything we could to alleviate her suffering in her last moments (oh Liesje, Liesje), we pooled all our wedding rings and gold fillings to buy her an egg, we stole and hoarded food to save her life, because her detail had been punished, they'd been forced for weeks to work while standing up to their waists in water—exhausted by pneumonia she collapsed and then when we'd managed to get her through the eye of the needle her detail was punished *again* and forced to stand to attention on the parade ground for hours, and now she's dead.

And Lea Lûbka's dead now, but I went back home and the radio was on and they were still reading out her name: Lea Lûbka, alive and well, is returning from the Mauthausen Concentration Camp. Your friend the painter.

And then there's the story of Nico Rost, who wears a cloth over his head to cover his sores, and about Dachau, where they carried a corpse into the food line with a mug in its hand so they could get a little more soup.

And the corpse consequently had to be present on parade.

And no one knew anything about the Resistance during the war, but four days after the liberation everyone's saying: I was in the Resistance. And now they're also already saying: I'm glad I was never in the Resistance, they were a bunch of fucking communists.

And my father says: we stuck a membership card from the Resistance in the shop window and now we hardly get any customers—and we threw someone out of the association of master painters because he'd worked with the Gestapo, and now the Gestapo man's already got a ration coupon for getting glass, and none of the painters who actually belong to the association have any coupons yet.

Stalpaert from the Recruiting Center

And in the station Stalpaert from the Recruiting Center is being transferred to prison in Gent and is standing waiting for the train surrounded by six gendarmes—and the news travels like wildfire: where where? Oh you bastard and this and that, punch him in the face, bravo. And he stands there expressionless. He has very pale lightless eyes that he focuses on a point which let's say is the station but can also be extended into infinity, and his head is red and purple from the beating he got yesterday. He's a head taller than everyone else as if he were the axis of a merry-go-round at a fair, and thump, the axis retreats, and thump the axis moves forward again while the merry-go-round of people goes on turning round him and shouting things at him that they've been saving up for four long years: wait till after the war!

Stalpaert look over here! says the gendarme, and so the storm flares up over here, laughing crying pale burning faces, one weeping and three blank. Well now, where are the days when we had to make way on the sidewalk for you and your missus, Mr. German Heil Hitler, Mr. idiot sadist cannibal. Hey Stalpaert look over there! says the gendarme, and then the storm flares up over there. And the stationmaster who's been standing and watching but hasn't said anything suddenly comes up waving his arms around: look out, the 7:45 train to Gent is coming. And where the outermost ring of the merry-go-round had been jostling to reach the axis suddenly they're all jostling each other trying not to get run over by the 7:45 train which comes thundering into the station—and looking for an empty compartment they trample over Stalpaert the axis, so that all of a sudden there's no more merry-go-round. Get in! says a gendarme, and Stalpaert gets in and looks for an empty corner with his uncomprehending eyes and sits down as if he's still Stalpaert from the Recruiting Center, as if he doesn't realize that Stalpaert from the Recruiting Center is a dream, a nightmare he had yesterday but that today is all over. Stalpaert stand up! says a gendarme and he stands at the train window with his arms raised, goddamn bastard, and the blood runs out of his nose onto his chin and drips onto his coat, his eyes still staring at that point in the distance. And standing there like that he's just like an image of Our Lord, Our Lord of the Devils! And a girl says: I'm going to faint—but she doesn't—and a gentleman starts talking in a pompous sort of way he's not used to: at last at last justice has been done.

And the train whistles and leaves, platform two is empty and platform three is full of people heading to Brussels and watching the Gent train as it pulls away. Someone looks down at his own sweaty palm in bewilderment and someone else who was in the inner circle of the merry-go-round just now says: I really don't like having to see things like that.

And there's Simonne and Lucette who want to go out dancing with the Canadians but have no room to dance and no room to sit and not even anyplace to stand, the whole room is full of schoolgirls of 14 and 15 with their asses and a lot more on show in the arms of old Canadians young Canadians drunk Canadians—but Jet who's an old whore of about sixty went to the dance too and only missed one dance and that was because she had to go out to use the toilet.

And the children who climb onto moving trucks and untie bags of coal and empty them off the back throw push one down with all their combined strength—and you think: how poor they must be—but if you follow the children you'll see that they sweep up all the spilled coal and manage to sell it at a premium somewhere.

And Maurice tells us about a fire somewhere and how a black American was at the top of the ladder and without even holding on to it rescued two children from their burning room—because those American blacks, THEY'RE TOO MUCH *says Maurice enthusiastically.*

And someone else tells me that some American blacks were billeted at a farm and the people there were so scared they moved their two young daughters out as fast as they could—and that the blacks raped the old farmer's wife so badly she died. Because those blacks, THEY'RE TOO MUCH, *real monsters, he says.*

And I have a chat with a policeman and he tells me how scared he is directing traffic on the corner of his avenue and the main Brussels road because those American blacks, THEY'RE TOO MUCH, *they're going to run over me one day.*

War Generation

Our generation blossomed between the two wars and we worshipped Romain Rolland the conscience of Europe and we shouted no-more-war in nighttime processions and had a woodcut by Masereel pinned on our wall (preferably the one of the kid with his hands tied behind his back who's about to be shot, and who with raised head is staring off at something Masereel didn't include in his woodcut) and at the movies we almost stamped a hole in the floorboards when they showed *Comradeship* by Pabst (oh when they knocked down the fence dividing the French and German miners as they ran to help each other!), and we said that the youth of our generation was the greatest there'd ever been . . .

But because we had the courage to belong to the youth-of-yesterday we should also have the courage to belong to the generation that's blossomed in this last war. The girls smoke one cigarette after another and drink whisky and tell the boys they're saving themselves for a Tommy, and the boys have gangly legs with knees that are a little too fat and wear swing jackets that are too long and pants that are too short with narrow legs and they all ate nothing but ration bread for four years. They heard the bombs falling and speak of the dead in the same tone as fallen leaves and swing and swing and swing. Mientje can cover the whole dance floor single-handed but then she's got the legs for it, young and beautiful, despite growing up in line for waste coal and herring in sun, rain, and wind. Oh they know damn well they'd better get paid if they're going to do something for someone, and they went on sitting in the milk bars where there was no more ice cream just artificial ice and they went to the movies where no one showed Pabst or Eisenstein anymore but the wonderful adventures of the German Baron von Münchhausen, in completely natural UFA color, and they thought it was incredible—yes, they did—and they love swing music but also loved those German films where people waltz and talk about swing like it's something barbaric—because they never think about anything, they just take everything they can get—but they still went on sitting bravely in their seats whenever the red warning letters started dancing on the white movie screen: air raid! It's an air raid! they said to the girl sitting next to them, as though she hadn't read it for herself.

But look, if you want to be one of these young people I should warn you that they're too matter-of-fact about everything. They can't live without a bit of romanticism in their lives but will always be sure to ask: how much is this bit of romanticism going to cost me? And they find all the things we dreamed about in our own youth completely ridiculous. But we don't have to retreat into a corner because of that—the hardest struggle in life is the struggle not to become bitter.

And suddenly a truck full of German POWs stops and everyone goes over to it with the bread and cigarettes that Belgium and America have paid through the nose for—and all the people who worked in Germany speak German to them, to show that they . . . well, that they what?—oh, those boys were so cold and so hungry in that truck, they say later. And there was a Belgian soldier there too, to guard them, but he didn't get anything, so I guess he wasn't cold or hungry. And when people hear a rumor that there's going to be less butter and no chocolate soon, they say indignantly: it's those awful Americans giving our food to the Germans!

And it's as if everyone is waiting for something to happen, says my brother-in-law—who's never done anything but wait.

Self-Defense

If I've usually said "I" in this book, it was just a way of presenting things, what I really meant was "you"—you, you poor man, exploited, scorned, spat upon, pacified with empty promises, who didn't have the courage or were too stupid to stand up for yourself, and who are laughing at me now and at this book because it shows you as you are and there's the occasional dirty word in it, haha. But let me talk about myself, really about myself, on this one rare occasion: I'd like to suggest to my publisher that he set up an "Everyone Write their Own Little War" contest—"First prize a pipe!"—so I can share my experiences and advice with all the entrants:

First and foremost the writer of a Little War has to believe that books are a form of public entertainment in which there can be no swearing or spitting on the ground and in which no one's sleeping conscience is ever startled awake. And then he has to remember that he needs to keep his eyes open at all times yet never write anything down as he actually sees it, because that isn't art—so the literary people tell us—that's just making yourself into a camera. And a writer has to be particularly careful not to walk down any dark alleys, since he might bump into someone who thinks he recognizes himself in Mr. Swaem the profiteer or that gentleman from the meat-inspection board or Proske or even What's-his-name himself. There are 36 people who think they're What's-his-name, and eleven gentlemen who give this particular writer angry looks whenever they walk by because they recognize themselves in Mr. Swaem—though he had only a symbolic Mr. Swaem in mind. Two of them wrote him threatening letters, five think they're Mr. Boone (because I'm fat, they say of themselves, and even though I don't live by a dump, the guy next door's always leaving his garbage cans out), four buttonholed the writer's wife cursing and swearing and saying they weren't going to take this slander lying down, and I threatened to come and personally drag him out from behind his desk. And then another gentleman asked for the names, places of birth, and occupations of a whole crowd of the writer's characters, as though he's always carrying a ledger round with him on his travels, so that everyone he wants to write about can come and sign in: I the undersigned hereby confirm . . . Just imagine if the railway asks me to supply the names and addresses of all the coal thieves, and as a result I'm forced to say: well, me on a small scale and you on a big one, Madame . . . And another gentleman writes an indignant letter: although I know you meant this in a humorous way, etc. etc. So you see a writer has to keep track of everything, keep thorough documentation and get it all notarized so no one can come up and accuse him of such patent falsehoods: dear sir, I swear I've never been humorous, next you'll be telling me you think Chaplin's denunciations of society are meant to be humorous too . . .

I bet you there'll be war again in less than ten years, someone says.

And someone else looks at him with fear in his eyes, fear at the thought of having to go through all that again—and now with the atom bomb . . .

And someone else again starts cursing those rotten . . . rotten . . . And finally shrugs his shoulders since he doesn't really know what's rotten.

And yet another person asks: but are you out of your MIND?

And now the very last one, who agrees with the first because he agrees with everyone, but who later on, in retrospect, says: I don't think it'll be as soon as that, because everything's been too smashed up—and he clings to that thought because THAT'S HIS CONSOLATION.

A last cry:

KICK PEOPLE HARD
TILL THEY GET A CONSCIENCE

Fifteen Years Later

And fifteen years later I'm crossing the station square with all sorts of things on my mind and I almost bump right into her. Something, I don't know what, makes me look at that bitter smile of hers. And immediately I drown in her eyes all over again. The years fall away. I see her again as she used to be, a child, helping us around the house . . .

They were very hard up in her house in those days and so after school she came to help my wife with all sorts of things. This help consisted mainly of breaking plates, getting thread tangled up, and unpicking wrongly stitched patches of cloth. She was still skinny then, her legs slightly too long, like an Easter lamb. But the most beautiful thing about her was her little face, a working-class girl with a furrow of hunger running round her mouth and eyes—things were at their worst then—along with a touch of refinement given to her by God knows who. I was desperately in love with her. If I'd still been a boy I would have sung her praises in verse—as it was I painted her on some hopelessly coarse wartime canvas. There she was sitting unpicking linen again for hours on end and meanwhile upsetting my wife with all kinds of questions. My wife was a product of the years when the world still believed all kinds of things, she joined associations and leagues and was filled with an unshakeable conviction that everything would really change one day. She would have been a perfect model for one of those prints where a mother is showing her child a great rising sun on the horizon—and in that sun some redeeming word, "Hope" or something.

Our little household helper on the other hand was a child of the war, one hundred percent. Bread, butter, coal, you had to stand in line for hours if you wanted them, you had to fight and sneak and plot. And at night there was the animal wail of the air-raid sirens in the air and you had to go down to the shelters. In our neighborhood these were just some hastily dug ditches with a few props and planks and the dug-up earth on top. Once upon a time heroes in helmets stood in the trenches, now it was children with worry lines round their eyes and mouths. And while she unpicked the wrongly sewn patches of material, she asked all kinds of devious questions that undermined my wife's faith. That was her real job, as it was for all war children: to hollow out, undermine, destroy.

And meanwhile, as I said, I was desperately and impossibly in love with her. And she knew, the little witch. She ate my ration of bread, butter, and meat. She put the food into her mouth tenderly and looked up at me and made me drown in the lakes of her eyes. She was barely twelve the first time she came to our house. And then later, when she was approaching eighteen, she began staying away for longer and longer periods of time. She'd been around for six long years, every night when I came home—a heaven and a hell: in the beginning more or less my daughter, eventually almost supplanting my wife. Then the young men started clinging to her like burrs—she was growing appallingly beautiful. And then the war was over and there was enough to eat and she simply didn't come around anymore. She was a child of our time. I hadn't seen her for years and didn't know where or what kind of life she was living.

Now I was crossing the station square, absorbed in my usual host of worries, and I recognized her at once. She was just then getting into her car and resting her hands on her steering wheel and suddenly she looked at me—just like then. She was wearing a fur coat. And again with that killer smile she put the car in gear and drove away, just like that, without so much as a hello. Some muddy water from a nearby puddle splashed over my pant legs.

And 15 years later I met Vieze again, my god what a shock, he'd become an old man from his battered feet to his baffled head. Right away I looked down at his blue-tattooed hands which had once been the terror of the female population, but could hardly see the anchors and suns anymore in all that crumpled skin. And worse yet, he didn't even recognize me.

I asked him if he still remembered this or still remembered that, and in a goddamn servile tone of voice he said: not that I know of, sir.

And again I remember the man who sent me an enthusiastic postcard when the first edition of this book appeared: I can't put down your Little War and I'll send you a longer letter later. And that was fifteen years ago now and I've never heard a thing from the guy, so that I constantly torment myself wondering whether he just dropped dead as he tried to finish my book.

Last Word

One mustn't speak ill of the dead—but I don't know if I can think up anything nice about Madame Ondine. She was a witch, that's what she was, whose only purpose in life was to pester and torment everyone, to make trouble, to be a bystander in war after war. What sort of poison was it that gnawed away at her insides, that made her act like that from morning till night, from the cradle to the grave? She had a real pushover of a husband who pined away in her shadow and then got drunk and ran wild once and a while, yelling from a safe distance that he was going to murder her. And she had wild children too that she tried to bring up to be saints but that she had to chase to bed without supper almost every day. She locked them upstairs and then went out gossiping round the neighborhood, running everyone down, like a comet towing a tail of hate and discord behind her.

And meanwhile those saintly monsters of hers set their little hovel on fire. She said: my children have been brought up respectably. Because respectability seemed to be the highest thing attainable in life—being respectable, being called a lady. And all her life she struggled frantically to get her paws on all the outward symbols of it, money, a bank account, a post office savings book. She never managed it. She didn't even have a single chair—however rickety—she could call her own. And there was one time she thought she'd really hit the jackpot, when the 1st World War was won-lost and the defeated German armies were withdrawing from the front in Flanders. I can still see them with my child's eyes—stumbling by, bleeding, filthy, in tattered uniforms. They sang of the *Krieg* that was over and the *Heimat* they were going to see again, and on their way they just threw away thousands and thousands of marks. No one else dared go out into the street. Only Madame Ondine, her uncombed hair hanging in strands, her bedraggled skirt covered in margarine stains, her stockings round her ankles, and her apron lifted up to hold the fluttering marks. Occasionally she would stop scrabbling around for a second to show heaven her apron stuffed full of notes and bare all her gray teeth in a grin. It later turned out that those marks were worthless, of course, that a million marks would hardly buy you a loaf of bread. She almost went crazy, they had to take her worthless fortune away by force and burn it in the courtyard.

Wait till there's war again! she said afterward. And she focused her husband and her wild children on the coming war that would make her dreams come true. The war came, and the youngest of her monsters was killed and the eldest became a blackshirt. And Ondine herself? By now she'd become old and gray and ill, and one day when she was lining up for who knows what, she collapsed. She died where she'd always lived, in the street.

But as her eyes clouded over she managed to say something very beautiful, something that can serve not only as *her* last word but also as the last word of this book:

WHAT'S THE POINT OF IT ALL?

Translator's Note

Louis Paul Boon's *My Little War* (*Mijn kleine oorlog*) has a three-stage publishing history.[1]

In 1947, seventeen stories, probably written in the first half of 1944, which had previously appeared in the magazine *Zondagspost* under the heading "Tales of the War," were expanded to over twice that number and published in book form as *My Little War*.

Thirteen years later, a revised and further expanded edition was published as a large-circulation paperback and went into many reprints. By this time, Boon—after sales in Flanders had proved disappointing—had joined the large Dutch publishing

---

1 The complete textual history of the book is traced and contextualized in K. Humbeeck et al., eds. *Louis Paul Boon. Mijn kleine oorlog.* Texteditie en nawoord. Amsterdam: Querido, 2002.

company De Arbeiderspers. On this occasion the author regularized the book's spelling and punctuation, toned down the Flemishness of its idiom, and bowdlerized some of its physical and sexual explicitness. Ironically, Boon's (successful) accommodation of a wider readership in the Netherlands attracted growing criticism in Flanders, where he was seen by many as compromising his youthful revolutionary principles. Significantly, the first edition was chosen for inclusion in Boon's uniform collected works (2005).

Without wishing to take sides on this vexed issue, I would like briefly to make a case for my choice of the 1960 edition for this translation. Firstly, it is the edition in which I, as a student, first encountered the book and the author, when its unique tone made an indelible impression. Moreover, it is the form in which the book was first presented to a wide reading public in the Netherlands and, I suspect, in Flanders itself. Secondly, the inclusion of the retrospective chapter "Fifteen Years Later" adds an elegiac dimension to the whole narrative, besides establishing a tantalizing link with the love triangle in Boon's compact masterpiece *Menuet* (1955). Indeed the whole book, without forfeiting its sense of outrage, has a more reflective cast than its predecessor. Finally, the 1960 text is, like it or not, the *Ausgabe letzter Hand*, the last edition corrected by the author himself.

I can appreciate the preference felt by some for the rough, uncut, "primitive" text of 1947. But while one may relish the directness of, say, Goethe's fragmentary *Urfaust*, especially in our post-expressionist world, the more mature structure of the revised and expanded *Faust, Der Tragödie erster Teil* surely has greater subtlety and complexity to offer readers, performers, and directors. The same, I would argue, is true of the revised second edition of *My Little War*. The possibly ideal solution of presenting both versions in English for reader to compare seems Utopian in today's publishing climate.

PAUL VINCENT

Louis Paul Boon's (1912–1979) oeuvre spans several genres, including historical epics, newspaper columns, and scabrous novels such as *Chapel Road* and *Summer in Termuren*.

Paul Vincent is an award-winning translator of Dutch literature whose translation of Hendrik Marsman's *Herinnering aan Holland* earned the David Reid Poetry Translation Prize.

SELECTED DALKEY ARCHIVE PAPERBACKS

PETROS ABATZOGLOU, *What Does Mrs. Freeman Want?*
MICHAL AJVAZ, *The Other City.*
PIERRE ALBERT-BIROT, *Grabinoulor.*
YUZ ALESHKOVSKY, *Kangaroo.*
FELIPE ALFAU, *Chromos.*
   Locos.
IVAN ÂNGELO, *The Celebration.*
   The Tower of Glass.
DAVID ANTIN, *Talking.*
ANTÓNIO LOBO ANTUNES, *Knowledge of Hell.*
ALAIN ARIAS-MISSON, *Theatre of Incest.*
JOHN ASHBERY AND JAMES SCHUYLER, *A Nest of Ninnies.*
HEIMRAD BÄCKER, *transcript.*
DJUNA BARNES, *Ladies Almanack.*
   Ryder.
JOHN BARTH, *LETTERS.*
   Sabbatical.
DONALD BARTHELME, *The King.*
   Paradise.
SVETISLAV BASARA, *Chinese Letter.*
MARK BINELLI, *Sacco and Vanzetti Must Die!*
ANDREI BITOV, *Pushkin House.*
LOUIS PAUL BOON, *Chapel Road.*
   My Little War.
   Summer in Termuren.
ROGER BOYLAN, *Killoyle.*
IGNÁCIO DE LOYOLA BRANDÃO, *Anonymous Celebrity.*
   Teeth under the Sun.
   Zero.
BONNIE BREMSER, *Troia: Mexican Memoirs.*
CHRISTINE BROOKE-ROSE, *Amalgamemnon.*
BRIGID BROPHY, *In Transit.*
MEREDITH BROSNAN, *Mr. Dynamite.*
GERALD L. BRUNS, *Modern Poetry and*
   the Idea of Language.
EVGENY BUNIMOVICH AND J. KATES, EDS.,
   Contemporary Russian Poetry: An Anthology.
GABRIELLE BURTON, *Heartbreak Hotel.*
MICHEL BUTOR, *Degrees.*
   Mobile.
   Portrait of the Artist as a Young Ape.
G. CABRERA INFANTE, *Infante's Inferno.*
   Three Trapped Tigers.
JULIETA CAMPOS, *The Fear of Losing Eurydice.*
ANNE CARSON, *Eros the Bittersweet.*
CAMILO JOSÉ CELA, *Christ versus Arizona.*
   The Family of Pascual Duarte.
   The Hive.
LOUIS-FERDINAND CÉLINE, *Castle to Castle.*
   Conversations with Professor Y.
   London Bridge.
   Normance.
   North.
   Rigadoon.
HUGO CHARTERIS, *The Tide Is Right.*
JEROME CHARYN, *The Tar Baby.*
MARC CHOLODENKO, *Mordechai Schamz.*
EMILY HOLMES COLEMAN, *The Shutter of Snow.*
ROBERT COOVER, *A Night at the Movies.*
STANLEY CRAWFORD, *Log of the S.S. The Mrs Unguentine.*
   Some Instructions to My Wife.
ROBERT CREELEY, *Collected Prose.*
RENÉ CREVEL, *Putting My Foot in It.*
RALPH CUSACK, *Cadenza.*
SUSAN DAITCH, *L.C.*
   Storytown.
NICHOLAS DELBANCO, *The Count of Concord.*
NIGEL DENNIS, *Cards of Identity.*
PETER DIMOCK, *A Short Rhetoric for Leaving the Family.*
ARIEL DORFMAN, *Konfidenz.*
COLEMAN DOWELL, *The Houses of Children.*
   Island People.
   Too Much Flesh and Jabez.
ARKADII DRAGOMOSHCHENKO, *Dust.*
RIKKI DUCORNET, *The Complete Butcher's Tales.*
   The Fountains of Neptune.
   The Jade Cabinet.
   The One Marvelous Thing.
   Phosphor in Dreamland.
   The Stain.
   The Word "Desire."
WILLIAM EASTLAKE, *The Bamboo Bed.*
   Castle Keep.
   Lyric of the Circle Heart.
JEAN ECHENOZ, *Chopin's Move.*
STANLEY ELKIN, *A Bad Man.*
   Boswell: A Modern Comedy.
   Criers and Kibitzers, Kibitzers and Criers.
   The Dick Gibson Show.
   The Franchiser.
   George Mills.
   The Living End.
   The MacGuffin.
   The Magic Kingdom.
   Mrs. Ted Bliss.
   The Rabbi of Lud.
   Van Gogh's Room at Arles.
ANNIE ERNAUX, *Cleaned Out.*
LAUREN FAIRBANKS, *Muzzle Thyself.*
   Sister Carrie.
JUAN FILLOY, *Op Oloop.*
LESLIE A. FIEDLER, *Love and Death in the American Novel.*

GUSTAVE FLAUBERT, *Bouvard and Pécuchet.*
KASS FLEISHER, *Talking out of School.*
FORD MADOX FORD, *The March of Literature.*
JON FOSSE, *Melancholy.*
MAX FRISCH, *I'm Not Stiller.*
   Man in the Holocene.
CARLOS FUENTES, *Christopher Unborn.*
   Distant Relations.
   Terra Nostra.
   Where the Air Is Clear.
JANICE GALLOWAY, *Foreign Parts.*
   The Trick Is to Keep Breathing.
WILLIAM H. GASS, *Cartesian Sonata and Other Novellas.*
   Finding a Form.
   A Temple of Texts.
   The Tunnel.
   Willie Masters' Lonesome Wife.
GÉRARD GAVARRY, *Hoppla! 1 2 3.*
ETIENNE GILSON, *The Arts of the Beautiful.*
   Forms and Substances in the Arts.
C. S. GISCOMBE, *Giscome Road.*
   Here.
   Prairie Style.
DOUGLAS GLOVER, *Bad News of the Heart.*
   The Enamoured Knight.
WITOLD GOMBROWICZ, *A Kind of Testament.*
KAREN ELIZABETH GORDON, *The Red Shoes.*
GEORGI GOSPODINOV, *Natural Novel.*
JUAN GOYTISOLO, *Count Julian.*
   Juan the Landless.
   Makbara.
   Marks of Identity.
PATRICK GRAINVILLE, *The Cave of Heaven.*
HENRY GREEN, *Back.*
   Blindness.
   Concluding.
   Doting.
   Nothing.
JIŘÍ GRUŠA, *The Questionnaire.*
GABRIEL GUDDING, *Rhode Island Notebook.*
JOHN HAWKES, *Whistlejacket.*
ALEKSANDAR HEMON, ED., *Best European Fiction 2010.*
AIDAN HIGGINS, *A Bestiary.*
   Balcony of Europe.
   Bornholm Night-Ferry.
   Darkling Plain: Texts for the Air.
   Flotsam and Jetsam.
   Langrishe, Go Down.
   Scenes from a Receding Past.
   Windy Arbours.
ALDOUS HUXLEY, *Antic Hay.*
   Crome Yellow.
   Point Counter Point.
   Those Barren Leaves.
   Time Must Have a Stop.
MIKHAIL IOSSEL AND JEFF PARKER, EDS., *Amerika:*
   Russian Writers View the United States.
GERT JONKE, *Geometric Regional Novel.*
   Homage to Czerny.
   The System of Vienna.
JACQUES JOUET, *Mountain R.*
   Savage.
CHARLES JULIET, *Conversations with Samuel Beckett and*
   Bram van Velde.
MIEKO KANAI, *The Word Book.*
HUGH KENNER, *The Counterfeiters.*
   Flaubert, Joyce and Beckett: The Stoic Comedians.
   Joyce's Voices.
DANILO KIŠ, *Garden, Ashes.*
   A Tomb for Boris Davidovich.
ANITA KONKKA, *A Fool's Paradise.*
GEORGE KONRÁD, *The City Builder.*
TADEUSZ KONWICKI, *A Minor Apocalypse.*
   The Polish Complex.
MENIS KOUMANDAREAS, *Koula.*
ELAINE KRAF, *The Princess of 72nd Street.*
JIM KRUSOE, *Iceland.*
EWA KURYLUK, *Century 21.*
ERIC LAURRENT, *Do Not Touch.*
VIOLETTE LEDUC, *La Bâtarde.*
SUZANNE JILL LEVINE, *The Subversive Scribe:*
   Translating Latin American Fiction.
DEBORAH LEVY, *Billy and Girl.*
   Pillow Talk in Europe and Other Places.
JOSÉ LEZAMA LIMA, *Paradiso.*
ROSA LIKSOM, *Dark Paradise.*
OSMAN LINS, *Avalovara.*
   The Queen of the Prisons of Greece.
ALF MAC LOCHLAINN, *The Corpus in the Library.*
   Out of Focus.
RON LOEWINSOHN, *Magnetic Field(s).*
BRIAN LYNCH, *The Winner of Sorrow.*
D. KEITH MANO, *Take Five.*
MICHELINE AHARONIAN MARCOM, *The Mirror in the Well.*
BEN MARCUS, *The Age of Wire and String.*
WALLACE MARKFIELD, *Teitlebaum's Window.*
   To an Early Grave.
DAVID MARKSON, *Reader's Block.*
   Springer's Progress.
   Wittgenstein's Mistress.
CAROLE MASO, *AVA.*

FOR A FULL LIST OF PUBLICATIONS, VISIT:
www.dalkeyarchive.com

SELECTED DALKEY ARCHIVE PAPERBACKS

LADISLAV MATEJKA AND KRYSTYNA POMORSKA, EDS.,
 Readings in Russian Poetics: Formalist and
 Structuralist Views.
HARRY MATHEWS,
 The Case of the Persevering Maltese: Collected Essays.
 Cigarettes.
 The Conversions.
 The Human Country: New and Collected Stories.
 The Journalist.
 My Life in CIA.
 Singular Pleasures.
 The Sinking of the Odradek Stadium.
 Tlooth.
 20 Lines a Day.
ROBERT L. MCLAUGHLIN, ED., *Innovations: An Anthology of*
 Modern & Contemporary Fiction.
HERMAN MELVILLE, *The Confidence-Man.*
AMANDA MICHALOPOULOU, *I'd Like.*
STEVEN MILLHAUSER, *The Barnum Museum.*
 In the Penny Arcade.
RALPH J. MILLS, JR., *Essays on Poetry.*
MOMUS, *The Book of Jokes.*
CHRISTINE MONTALBETTI, *Western.*
OLIVE MOORE, *Spleen.*
NICHOLAS MOSLEY, *Accident.*
 Assassins.
 Catastrophe Practice.
 Children of Darkness and Light.
 Experience and Religion.
 God's Hazard.
 The Hesperides Tree.
 Hopeful Monsters.
 Imago Bird.
 Impossible Object.
 Inventing God.
 Judith.
 Look at the Dark.
 Natalie Natalia.
 Paradoxes of Peace.
 Serpent.
 Time at War.
 The Uses of Slime Mould: Essays of Four Decades.
WARREN MOTTE,
 Fables of the Novel: French Fiction since 1990.
 Fiction Now: The French Novel in the 21st Century.
 Oulipo: A Primer of Potential Literature.
YVES NAVARRE, *Our Share of Time.*
 Sweet Tooth.
DOROTHY NELSON, *In Night's City.*
 Tar and Feathers.
WILFRIDO D. NOLLEDO, *But for the Lovers.*
FLANN O'BRIEN, *At Swim-Two-Birds.*
 At War.
 The Best of Myles.
 The Dalkey Archive.
 Further Cuttings.
 The Hard Life.
 The Poor Mouth.
 The Third Policeman.
CLAUDE OLLIER, *The Mise-en-Scène.*
PATRIK OUŘEDNÍK, *Europeana.*
FERNANDO DEL PASO, *News from the Empire.*
 Palinuro of Mexico.
ROBERT PINGET, *The Inquisitory.*
 Mahu or The Material.
 Trio.
MANUEL PUIG, *Betrayed by Rita Hayworth.*
 Heartbreak Tango.
RAYMOND QUENEAU, *The Last Days.*
 Odile.
 Pierrot Mon Ami.
 Saint Glinglin.
ANN QUIN, *Berg.*
 Passages.
 Three.
 Tripticks.
ISHMAEL REED, *The Free-Lance Pallbearers.*
 The Last Days of Louisiana Red.
 The Plays.
 Reckless Eyeballing.
 The Terrible Threes.
 The Terrible Twos.
 Yellow Back Radio Broke-Down.
JEAN RICARDOU, *Place Names.*
RAINER MARIA RILKE,
 The Notebooks of Malte Laurids Brigge.
JULIÁN RÍOS, *Larva: A Midsummer Night's Babel.*
 Poundemonium.
AUGUSTO ROA BASTOS, *I the Supreme.*
OLIVIER ROLIN, *Hotel Crystal.*
JACQUES ROUBAUD, *The Form of a City Changes Faster,*
 Alas, Than the Human Heart.
 The Great Fire of London.
 Hortense in Exile.
 Hortense Is Abducted.
 The Loop.
 The Plurality of Worlds of Lewis.
 The Princess Hoppy.
 Some Thing Black.
LEON S. ROUDIEZ, *French Fiction Revisited.*

VEDRANA RUDAN, *Night.*
STIG SÆTERBAKKEN, *Siamese.*
LYDIE SALVAYRE, *The Company of Ghosts.*
 Everyday Life.
 The Lecture.
 Portrait of the Writer as a Domesticated Animal.
 The Power of Flies.
LUIS RAFAEL SÁNCHEZ, *Macho Camacho's Beat.*
SEVERO SARDUY, *Cobra & Maitreya.*
NATHALIE SARRAUTE, *Do You Hear Them?*
 Martereau.
 The Planetarium.
ARNO SCHMIDT, *Collected Stories.*
 Nobodaddy's Children.
CHRISTINE SCHUTT, *Nightwork.*
GAIL SCOTT, *My Paris.*
DAMION SEARLS, *What We Were Doing and*
 Where We Were Going.
JUNE AKERS SEESE,
 Is This What Other Women Feel Too?
 What Waiting Really Means.
BERNARD SHARE, *Inish.*
 Transit.
AURELIE SHEEHAN, *Jack Kerouac Is Pregnant.*
VIKTOR SHKLOVSKY, *Knight's Move.*
 A Sentimental Journey: Memoirs 1917–1922.
 Energy of Delusion: A Book on Plot.
 Literature and Cinematography.
 Theory of Prose.
 Third Factory.
 Zoo, or Letters Not about Love.
JOSEF ŠKVORECKÝ, *The Engineer of Human Souls.*
CLAUDE SIMON, *The Invitation.*
GILBERT SORRENTINO, *Aberration of Starlight.*
 Blue Pastoral.
 Crystal Vision.
 Imaginative Qualities of Actual Things.
 Mulligan Stew.
 Pack of Lies.
 Red the Fiend.
 The Sky Changes.
 Something Said.
 Splendide-Hôtel.
 Steelwork.
 Under the Shadow.
W. M. SPACKMAN, *The Complete Fiction.*
ANDRZEJ STASIUK, *Fado.*
GERTRUDE STEIN, *Lucy Church Amiably.*
 The Making of Americans.
 A Novel of Thank You.
PIOTR SZEWC, *Annihilation.*
GONÇALO M. TAVARES, *Jerusalem.*
LUCIAN DAN TEODOROVICI, *Our Circus Presents . . .*
STEFAN THEMERSON, *Hobson's Island.*
 The Mystery of the Sardine.
 Tom Harris.
JEAN-PHILIPPE TOUSSAINT, *The Bathroom.*
 Camera.
 Monsieur.
 Running Away.
 Television.
DUMITRU TSEPENEAG, *Pigeon Post.*
 The Necessary Marriage.
 Vain Art of the Fugue.
ESTHER TUSQUETS, *Stranded.*
DUBRAVKA UGRESIC, *Lend Me Your Character.*
 Thank You for Not Reading.
MATI UNT, *Brecht at Night.*
 Diary of a Blood Donor.
 Things in the Night.
ÁLVARO URIBE AND OLIVIA SEARS, EDS.,
 The Best of Contemporary Mexican Fiction.
ELOY URROZ, *The Obstacles.*
LUISA VALENZUELA, *He Who Searches.*
PAUL VERHAEGHEN, *Omega Minor.*
MARJA-LIISA VARTIO, *The Parson's Widow.*
BORIS VIAN, *Heartsnatcher.*
ORNELA VORPSI, *The Country Where No One Ever Dies.*
AUSTRYN WAINHOUSE, *Hedyphagetica.*
PAUL WEST, *Words for a Deaf Daughter & Gala.*
CURTIS WHITE, *America's Magic Mountain.*
 The Idea of Home.
 Memories of My Father Watching TV.
 Monstrous Possibility: An Invitation to
 Literary Politics.
 Requiem.
DIANE WILLIAMS, *Excitability: Selected Stories.*
 Romancer Erector.
DOUGLAS WOOLF, *Wall to Wall.*
 Ya! & John-Juan.
JAY WRIGHT, *Polynomials and Pollen.*
 The Presentable Art of Reading Absence.
PHILIP WYLIE, *Generation of Vipers.*
MARGUERITE YOUNG, *Angel in the Forest.*
 Miss MacIntosh, My Darling.
REYOUNG, *Unbabbling.*
ZORAN ŽIVKOVIĆ, *Hidden Camera.*
LOUIS ZUKOFSKY, *Collected Fiction.*
SCOTT ZWIREN, *God Head.*